Classics of Modern Chinese Literature

A Bing Xin Reader

Translated by Zhao Yuan
Illustrated by Jia Xiaoxi

 CHINA INTERCONTINENTAL PRESS

图书在版编目（CIP）数据

冰心：英文 / 冰心著；

赵元译 .—— 北京：五洲传播出版社 ,2013.11

（中国儿童名著精选译丛）

ISBN 978-7-5085-2651-5

Ⅰ . ①冰… Ⅱ . ①冰… ②赵… Ⅲ . ①儿童文学－作

品综合集－中国－现代－英文 Ⅳ . ①I286

中国版本图书馆CIP数据核字(2013)第257181号

出 版 人：荆孝敏

作　　者：冰　心

译　　者：赵　元

插 图 作 者：贾晓曦

责 任 编 辑：张美景

装 帧 设 计：缪　惟

出版发行：五洲传播出版社

社　　址：北京市海淀区北三环中路31号生产力大楼B座7层

邮政编码：100088

发行电话：010-82005927, 010-82007837

网　　址：www.cicc.org.cn

制版单位：北京锦绣圣艺文化发展有限公司

印　　刷：北京天颖印刷有限公司

开　　本：889mmx1094mm　1/32

印　　张：6.5

版　　次：2013年11月第1版　2013年11月第1次印刷

书　　号：ISBN 978-7-5085-2651-5

定　　价：89.00元

contents

Introduction

Fu Lei, a great translator, wrote in one of his family letters to his son Fou Ts'ong:

I have always borne in mind "the heart of a newborn babe." A newborn babe doesn't know what loneliness is. If it is lonely, it will create a world and many friends of the soul. Keep the heart of a newborn babe forever, and you will never fall behind the ranks, even when you are old, and you will be able to empathize and connect with the innocent hearts throughout the world at any time. That friend of yours is right in saying that the efficacy of artistic expression must stem from the purity of one's heart. How can you have a true understanding of the souls of your predecessors, and how can you touch the souls of your audience, if your heart is not as pure as a bright mirror?

Although not indispensable for every one of us in our lives, childlike innocence is certainly necessary for a person engaged in artistic creation.

Bing Xin, the author of this collection, enjoyed a worldwide reputation as a prolific writer and one of the pioneers of children's literature in modern China. Her works fully embody her philosophy of love – maternal love, love of children, and love of nature.

Born Xie Wanying on Oct. 5, 1900 into a patriotic family in Fujian Province, Bing Xin had a really happy childhood. It was during the May Fourth Movement that she began writing. After graduating from Yenching University in 1923 with a bachelor's degree, Bing Xin went to the United States for further study in literature at Wellesley College. After she returned to China in 1926, she began teaching at Yenching University until 1936. Bing Xin's literary career spanned over seventy years, and her most well-known works include *A Myriad of Stars*, *Spring Waters*, and *Letters to Young Readers*.

This selection of Bing Xin's writings for children is comprised of a selection (about a half) of *Letters to Young Readers*, the first four letters in *More Letters to Young Readers*, and six short pieces which include Bing Xin's best-known short story "The Little Orange Lamp."

During her stay in the United States, Bing Xin wrote a lot about what she experienced and thought there, and then contributed what she wrote to newspapers. These prose pieces were later published under the title of *Letters to Young Readers* in 1926. Perhaps no one has described the beautiful things in a war-torn world better than Bing Xin. *More Letters to Young Readers*, written during the Anti-Japanese war, is filled with bright sunshine, precious friendship, gratitude towards mothers, and the awe of life, which brought love and hope to the Chinese young readers at that time.

In her earliest years, Bing Xin was exposed to traditional Chinese literature, and her favorite works were *The Romance of the Three Kingdoms*, *A Journey to the West*, and *The Outlaws of the Marsh*. She said she knew the plots and the characters' names in those novels thoroughly. We can imagine how excited she was when, for the first time in her life, she went to a Beijing opera theater with her parents and saw her favorite characters walk onto the stage one by one in splendid costumes. Her enthusiasm for Beijing opera never faded. In 1959, Bing Xin had an opportunity to visit a Beijing opera school. The children who were learning Beijing opera there were praiseworthy because they were hard-working and self-disciplined. Bing Xin hoped that they "perform on the stage the historical stories of life and struggle and the familiar characters that the people love to see in a more vivid and powerful way."

The Spring Festival is one of the most significant festivals for the Chinese, but nowadays many people complain that they can't enjoy the authentic traditional Chinese New Year. What is the true meaning of the Spring Festival, then? In "The Spring Festivals in my Childhood," Bing Xin presents us with the traditional customs of the Spring Festival in Yantai, Shangdong Province and Fuzhou, Fujian Province.

Bing Xin not only loved the world but felt sympathy for the lower-classes. In "Separation," the two babies, born at the same time and in the same place, are separated from each other owing to difference in class. Bing Xin's dissatisfaction and indignation about the unfair society is evident in this heartrending story.

In "Good Mother," a piece with a strong flavor of everyday life, we see a variation of the theme of love for mothers. At the beginning of the story, the speaker, a middle school girl student, has grumbles against her mother. After a visit to their neighbor's, however, she realizes that she is wrong and that she has a really good mother.

Of all the characters in Bing Xin's stories, the most impressive one must be the little girl in "The Little Orange Lamp." The delicate lamp she makes out of a big orange, as well as her calmness, courage, and optimism, provides infinite light for the narrator to move on.

In order for the reader to actually see the dances of the Indian sisters, Bing Xin employed various writing techniques. The result is spectacular, although she asserted that she could only describe their performance "in flat, monotonous language."

When reading Bing Xin's works, you feel as if she were sitting before you and showing you a painting which portrays her life experiences. She talks about such immortal things as love, good, and truth, but she never teaches you explicitly what to do or how to do it. Nevertheless, you can draw encouragement from her insights about life.

Bing Xin's writings have been incorporated into children's textbooks, and every primary school and high school student in China has read at least one of her pieces. I still remember a sentence from one of her letters to young readers, which I came across in my school years: "I dare not say what life is; I can only say what life is like." In that letter, Bing Xin used figurative language to describe vividly what life is like to children, who have not had many experiences about life yet.

Finally, I want to add that every book has a life of its own and that we should read a book as a person. Imagine this situation: when a stranger comes towards you with a smile on his face, how will you respond then? Will you return a smile or walk past him indifferently? Of course, the "stranger" refers to a book, and the "smile" its idea. As a book invites you to read it, how you react to it depends entirely on you. If you think of it only as a conveyer of information, you are reading a book passively. Instead, if you treat a book as a living thinker, with whom you can exchange ideas, then it belongs to you entirely at that very moment. Needless to say, a great work always resonates with its readers. And I do believe that you will have a very pleasant conversation with this little book, which is pregnant with love, joy, innocence, and kindness – things we all need to become better persons and to have better lives.

Li Yu

Letters to Young Readers
(A Selection)

Letter 1

July 25th, 1923

Dear little friends whom I seem to have met before,

As I am in bad health and am going on a long journey, I have thought that, for the next two or three months, I will have to stop writing anything. However, when I saw yesterday that the Morning Post supplement had started a special column called "Children's World," I was so joyful that I set myself, notwithstanding my weak wrist and rusty writing, to correspond with my dear little friends for the first time.

Please permit me, in this very first letter, to introduce myself to you. I am one of those who fall behind in your innocent group. There is one thing, however, that I am very proud of; that is, I was once a child and sometimes I still am. In order to retain that innocence until I go on to another world, I sincerely hope that you guide and help me. Of course, I will always urge myself to be one of the most passionate and faithful friends of yours.

Little friends, I am leaving for a place

very far from home. I am looking forward to it very much, because traveling may provide me with a lot of material so that I can tell you new things in my following letters. The place I am going to is on the other side of the earth. I have three younger brothers, the smallest of whom is thirteen years old. He has learned enough geography to know that the earth is round. He said to me jokingly, "Sister, if we miss you when you are away, we can poke a hole with a very long bamboo pole to connect our yards, so we can see each other. I'd like to see if you have gained or lost weight." Little friends, do you think it possible? There is another little friend in my family who is four this year. One day he asked me, "Auntie, is the place you are going to farther than the Front Gate?" Little friends, which do you think is farther, the other side of the world or the Front Gate?

I am leaving — away from my parents and brothers, away from all those I love. I feel very sad, although it won't be long before I come back. If you — on a breezy morning or a rainy evening, in the company of your parents and siblings, or when you are having a happy time — could think of me, a most passionate and loyal friend of yours, who will be tens of thousands of miles away in dreadful weather and unable to enjoy such happiness as yours, then a mere innocent thought of yours from afar, by virtue of the spirit of the universe, would give me infinite blessing and consolation.

Little friends, provided I have time, I will not allow the correspondence between us to cease for long. If the interval is a bit too long, please forgive me, for unless I put pen to paper the moment I regain a child's heart, I dare not write to you with the vexed mind of an adult. This I beg you to understand and pity.

It is about time to bring this letter to conclusion. I have an unspeakable feeling in my heart, but certainly I feel deeply honored.

Yours,
Bing Xin

Letter 2

July 28th, 1923

Dear little friends,

I am extremely unwilling to tell you, at the beginning of the second letter, a saddest story. However, it has made my soul suffer so much since last year that I cannot but repent now in front of my pure little friends.

It was a spring night last year — a leisurely night indeed — and it was after nine. My younger brothers having gone to bed, my father and mother were sitting opposite each other at the round table, reading, eating refreshments and talking. Standing against the back of a chair, I was reading a book too. All was gentle and quiet.

A little mouse sneaked from under the table and began nibbling slowly at the crumbs on the ground. It was a very small mouse; it ate away calmly and innocently, raising its head to look at me from time to time. I cried out both in surprise and for joy, and my parents looked down. Stared at from all sides, the mouse remained there contented. By the dim light of the lamp, we could see its tiny nimble body, delicate light grey hair, and sparkling little eyes.

Little friends, please allow me to repent! At that moment, I was out of my wits. I bent down and covered it gently with my book. Good Heavens! It didn't move. I could feel through the pages its soft body curling up, unresisting, on the ground.

That was completely out of my expectations. I was pressing its little hand, which was trembling, when my mother said, "Why are you doing this? What a tame and interesting little thing..." She hadn't finished yet when Huer, our puppy, jumped in from outside the door screen. Father said hastily, "Loose it, or Huer'll get it!" I was out of my wits again and took away my book — how I regretted it! The mouse, however, kept still and contented. With a muffled groan of joy, Huer sprang on the mouse and, before I could stop him, went out through the curtain with his prey between his teeth. From out of the door came a few faint piteous cries from inside Huer's mouth, but before long no sound could be heard. Within a minute, the poor little thing pierced my heart as if it had been hit by an arrow.

When the panic was over, I sighed a deep sigh. Mother put down her book, raised her head and said to me, "It must be too small and too naïve; otherwise, it would have escaped. It went out to look for food for the first time. When its mother found her child hadn't gone back, it's hard to imagine how she would miss it."

Little friends, I have degenerated, really. If I had been your age, I would, at these words, have moved slowly toward my mother and, throwing myself into her arms, cried bitterly. At that time, however, I... Please forgive me, little friends! I pretended to be indifferent and smiled.

When it was time to go to bed, I went back to my bedroom. An assumed smile only added to my sin. I paced up and down, not knowing what to do – I didn't change

clothes; leaning against the edge of my bed and bending over the pillow, I kept silent for fifteen minutes. Then, I wept, at last.

A year has passed. Sometimes, when I work late into the night and see a mouse coming out, I inevitably feel so sad and ashamed that I have the impulse to shun it. I always have the impression that it is the mother of that little mouse, who goes out every night, with tears of sadness in her eyes, to look for her child.

What's more, I think of that when I see Huer and when I wake up at night. Indeed, that

impression tortures my heart from time to time. Once, that torture became so intolerable that I confessed it to an adult friend. I had prepared to be bombarded by her so that my pain could be eased to some extent. To my surprise, she laughed and said, "You have grown more and more childish. What's so big about such a trivial matter?" The indifferent smile on her face prevented me from saying what I had intended to tell her. From then on, I lost heart completely and never told a second adult about that "trivial matter."

When I was a child, I wept for a cricket which had broken its leg and bewailed a wounded siskin. At that time, I knew that all forms of life were equal in the eye of the Creator; when I was young, I did nothing inhumane, but now I have degenerated...

Today, I confess everything to you, my impartial little friends, for your judgment.

Yours in Beijing,
Bing Xin

Letter 6

August 16th, 1923

Little friends,

When you are reading this, I will have been on a ship in the Pacific, away from my beloved motherland, which is in the shape of a begonia leaf. Today I am not in the mood for sentimental words; I will say nothing of it to stir up your unsophisticated mind.

Little friends, I have a suggestion. As "Children's World" is meant for children, i.e., written by children for children, why don't we move steadily forward and try our best to occupy this area. If you have a happy or funny story, share it with all other children so that they laugh with you; if you have a sad story, share it with all other children so that they shed tears with you. Just be frank and confident; there's no need to flinch from adults. Little friends, as it is our secret, let's share it here in secret. Adults' thoughts are too profound for us to fathom. I don't understand why their sense of right and wrong is vastly different from ours. What we grieve or are indignant over they respond with cheerful nonchalance; what we regard as an insignificant matter they esteem as an earth-shaking feat. For instance, on hearing (for there is no need to see it) that tens of thousands of people are injured or killed in war and lie on the ground badly mangled, we are so scared that at night we either are sleepless or talk in our sleep. Adults, however, don't care about that at all; what's more, they like to manipulate such things. Also, we don't care who becomes the president of our country, as long as he is honest, governs justly, grants us peace and safety, and does not hinder our play. But adults go about discussing it heatedly, electing this guy or that guy. What an awful mess! It is even more troublesome than electing "kid-in-chief" in our games. Anyway, we don't dare mind their business, nor do we desire to. As for our business, they don't think it worth minding. So, we may safely have a pleasant talk together and have no worry about their ridiculing us. — That's all I want to say. Little friends, please clap your hands in approval!

As for myself, I'm afraid you won't hear from me for the next two months, owing to the delay of letters on the way, except for the ones I might send from Japan in a week. As the autumn wind is getting chillier, it is now the best season to practice writing. I hope you work hard.

There are many more interesting things in Shanghai that I'd like to share with you, if I'm not so busy. I'll have to save them for a later time, probably when I'm on the sea. Please be patient.

Little friends, I'm leaving tomorrow afternoon. May God's generous, loving light shine upon us forever and comfort us forever.

Adieu, adieu! My final words to you: try to be good boys and girls!

Yours in Shanghai,

Bing Xin

Letter 7

August 20th, 1923

Dear little friends,

On the afternoon of August 17th, when I saw colorful streamers flying out of the innumerable portholes of the ocean liner Yorkson and landing on the retreating shore, allowing themselves to be caught by people who came to see off those who were departing, how restless and grieved I was!

There were countless people on the shore, broken streamers in hand and all in a trance-like state. They gazed after the ever-receding gigantic ship sailing westward, loaded down with the sorrow of parting.

Daily life on the ship was refreshing and active. Apart from the three meals, I played games and took walks as I pleased. For the first three days on the sea, I seemed to become a child once more. I was absorbed in tossing rings and throwing beanbags but, like a child, once the games were over I wouldn't play them ever again. When I recalled this episode later, I thought it was really odd. The only explanation was that the sea evoked memories of my childhood and, amidst the sound of waves, a child's playfulness and the images of my playmates all sprang into my mind. How I wish there had been some children on board on those three days when playfulness revisited me, so that I could play innocent games to my heart's content!

Although I grew up near the sea, I had

never seen such a sea surface before; it was as smooth as a mirror. Once we were out of the Wusong estuary, for a whole day, what we could see was small glistening undulations stretching to the horizon. The breeze was gentle, and the ship slid along as if on ice. After we were past the Korean waters, the sea turned out to be very much like a lake, with its body of water condensed into exceeding blue and green. The golden rays of the setting sun, like long snakes, shot up from the horizon right at the railings at which some people were standing. From the firmament down to the waters just in front of our ship, there was a spectrum of shades of colors, from light pink to dark green, rippling in layers and patches. ...Little friends, what a pity it is that I can't paint! I find that words are utterly worthless, for they are incapable of describing such ethereal beauty as I saw at that time.

The evening of August 18th was the time when the Herd-boy and the Weaving-girl were supposed to meet. After supper, I leaned over the railings, clothes fluttering in the cool breeze. The dark sea was illuminated by the starlight from the Milky Way. The sound of human voices and laughter came floating up from the distant railings down below. It suddenly dawned on me that I was getting farther and farther away from home. Stars twinkling in the sky, waves roaring underneath, I stood there all alone, consumed with melancholy.

At dusk on the 19th, we were approaching Kobe. There were green hills on both shores, and fishing boats were seen coming and going.

Most hills in Japan were round-topped and we jokingly called them "steamed-bun hills." The steamed-bun hills dotted the shores until night fell, when we spotted myriads of light in the distance. We were arriving at Kobe. No sooner had the ship moored than many people began to disembark. As it was late at night, I went up alone to the topmost deck. For the first time in my life, I saw such a resplendent scene: the light from the crescent moon, the stars, and the lamps on the shore added radiance and beauty to each other. Now and then, a string of light sailed across the hills — perhaps it was a train going round. ...The ship was silent, and no sound of the tidal waves could be heard tonight. Out of this utter silence suddenly arose the idea, "If only Mother were here now..." and the unmistakable image of Beijing leaped into my mind. Please forgive me, little friends. I have to stop here.

Yours in Kobe,
Bing Xin

Letter 8

Beebe Hall, Wellesley College
October 24th, 1923. Night

Dear younger brothers,

It has been raining for days this autumn in Boston. It seems that the weather will never clear up. The fallen leaves, yellow and red in color, are piling up on the paths, already an inch deep. When stepped on, the leaves feel wet and soft under the feet. I go to the lake less frequently, but at least once a day. On the long and quiet path I walk alone, listening to the sound of rain falling on my umbrella. Sometimes, I laugh at myself and wonder why I come and go like this all alone, braving the elements. When I get to the lake, the rocks and tree stumps are all wet and there is nowhere to sit. So I have to stand for a while, looking at the fine mist. The surface of the lake is a vast expanse of the faintest whiteness, and the trees on the shores are invisible. It is impossible to tell how large the lake is, which lends a sense of mystery to it.

When I get back, it is already quite late. I draw the green curtain, turn on the lamp, and start to read ancient Chinese poetry and the newly arrived Morning Post Supplements. When I come across words that I sympathize with, I nearly forget that I am in a foreign country and, on hearing a knock at the door, I will utter "Qing jin" involuntarily. Turning my head, I find a girl with blue eyes and blond hair standing there smiling and illuminated by the brightly-lit lamp overhead. This scene will bring me back to reality immediately, which is followed by laughing and sighing.

I have no idea how Beijing is faring and how China is faring. I wonder why I didn't show as much concern as when I was home. On one morning a couple of days ago, I sat on a rock by the lake, reading a poem by Wordsworth,

"I Travelled among Unknown Men":

I Travelled among Unknown Men

I travelled among unknown men,
In land beyond the sea,
Nor, England! did I know till then
What love I bore to thee.

Reading this, I seemed to suddenly realize something and, at the same time, I felt I was somewhat lost. Unknown, indeed! Returning from the lake, I saw, from afar, clusters of lights, as splendid as stars, from the windows of buildings, but they failed to bring me any comfort.

I recalled that, in this season, the streets in Beijing are resonant with the shouts of grape vendors and date vendors. Back at home, I, being a vulnerable person, used to be moved by the plaintive and stirring sound of their shouts mixed with the autumn wind, which woke me from my

nap. It was a Sunday afternoon, if my mind doesn't fail me, and you had gone boating somewhere outside the Gate of Stability. I sat on the porch alone, and the chill autumn wind cut right through me. The shouts of a date vendor were heard from outside the wall, which dampened my spirits. I was wondering why I was so lonely when the sounds of your cheerful chatting and laughter reached my ears from the other side of the wall. And instantly, my melancholy was gone. From then on, I confessed that you were my comfort and source of happiness, and I came to understand that, as long as one had the spirit of spring in one's mind, the autumn wind would not make one sorrowful. However, I never told you that, until today when it occurred to me again. There are no shouts of selling grapes and sweet dates, and it is raining and blowing hard outside. For the sake of life, I had to depart from you all, but I couldn't bear the departing. How will you comfort me? ...Twice a day, I go downstairs, key in hand, to check my mailbox, with a mixed feeling of worry and expectation.

Looking through the transparent glass, I can't find even a scrap of paper. I looked more closely at it; there is nothing in there. Listlessly, I drag my feet upstairs. This has happened more than once! I know it's impossible to receive letters every day, we being tens of thousands of miles apart; however, I can't persuade myself to quit the two errands each day. With what will you comfort me?

The nights are getting longer; it's time for study. I'd like to encourage you all, who are on the other side of the earth, to set aside some time after supper, as I do, for study. However, I'm afraid that you probably are in the classroom while I'm working under the lamp. When you are back from school, do try to spend more time with Mother! Time spent with Mother is dearer than gold, don't take it lightly. You can't imagine how your sister envies you! When I was home, I could concentrate on reading and writing at night and didn't need to bother about when to go to bed, because when it was about time, Father or Mother would come to remind me.

I would put down my pen and give them a smile. That was the happiest moment. Now, when it's getting late and I'm tired, I can do nothing but languidly put things in order and then dream about going home. Brothers! Think about me, and you will see the importance of enjoying as much as you can the life you are having now.

Chrysanthemums are in season now; presumably, Father is getting busy again. Did you raise many this year? I only have a daffodil on my desk. It's still in bud. As long as it is in bud, there is hope. I should have enough reason to feel joyful.

It's about time to have supper. American girls love to dress up, especially in the evening. As soon as the bells ring for the first time, they start to get dressed and apply cosmetics. Every evening, they appear at the dining tables, all gorgeously decorated. "Her dimples are rare, her eyes dark and lucid; those beauties are from the West." Once I playfully translated these lines from The Book of Poetry for them. They gathered around me and listened attentively. Having heard my words, they looked at each other and laughed out loud.

I may just stop here. Do take care!

Yours,
Bing Xin
P.S. If you'd like to, you may share this letter with our little friends. I'm still sorting out the letters I wrote on the journey, and I can't possibly mail them within one or two days. So, this one may serve as a filler; after all, a little comfort is better than none.

Letter 10

Simpson Infirmary, Wellesley
December 5th, 1923. Morning

Dear little friends,

I loved to sit by my mother, tugging at her sleeve, and nag her to tell me stories about my childhood.

Thinking for a while, Mother smiled and said softly:

"When you were only three months old, you had many diseases. When you heard the footsteps of the person who brought you medicine, you already knew what was going to happen and cried in fear. Many people were gathering around your bed, and you looked pitifully at no one but me, as if you had already recognized your mother from the crowd."

With those words, tears welled up in our eyes.

"On the day when you were just one month old, you were wearing clothes made of bright pink silk, which were given as a gift by your aunt, and a scarlet hat with a black satin hatband. I took you in my arms and went to the hall. Looking at your chubby, ruddy cheeks, I felt very proud among my sisters and sisters-in-law.

"When you were only seven months old, I held you in my arms and stood by the railings on an ocean liner. We could hear you crying out 'mama' and 'sister' above the sound of the waves."

Over this, Father and Mother frequently got into a dispute. Father didn't believe there was ever a child in the world who could speak when only seven months old. Mother insisted. So far, this event has remained a mystery in the history of our family.

"You were sleeping soundly when the voice of some female beggars woke you up. You thought your mother had been taken away by them and sat up in alarm. Your face was soaked in cold sweat, both your cheeks and lips turned green, and your voice was choked with sobs. I hastily came in from the backroom and held you tight in my arms. It took infinite explanation and consoling to calm you down. From then on, I stayed at your bedside as much as I could, even when you had fallen asleep."

I have a dim memory of that episode. When I heard it for the second time, I couldn't help but start sobbing. Indeed, while I'm writing about this now, I start sobbing again.

"Once, you were very ill. I held you in my arms and moved about on my knees on the mat on the floor. It was summer, and your father was not home. You uttered a few words now and then, words that a child of three was not capable of saying. The manifestation of extraordinary wisdom on your part gave me an undefinable feeling of terror. I sent a telegram to your father, saying I could no longer hold out, both physically and mentally. A heavy storm broke. You, who were seriously ill, I, who was deeply worried, and your exhausted wet nurse all fell into a sound sleep. This storm snatched you from the arms of Death.''

I don't believe I am wise, but meanwhile I don't doubt it. My mother's wisdom enabled her to regard everything as a manifestation of wisdom, let alone her only dearest daughter.

"I had great trouble braiding your hair in the morning, because your hair was not long enough and you wouldn't keep still even for a moment. When I was at my wit's end, your father would come to my rescue. He would say to you, "Stand still, girl. I'm taking a photo of you." He pretended to be taking photos, camera in hand. Two short and thick braids, done with difficulty every day."

I wonder why I didn't ask my father for the photos he took every day.

"Nanny Chen's daughter, Bao, was your good friend. When she came, I would lock you two in the room and then take a nap. When I woke up, all the toys, the little men and horses, were converted into boats, floating in the basin filled with water, and the floor was all wet."

Bao is a mysterious friend of mine, for I can remember nothing about her, nor do I know her. However, I have taken to her deeply based on what Mother has said about her.

"You were already three years old, or approaching four. Your father was going to take you to his warship, and we hastened to dress you. You put a wooden deer into your little boot without our noticing it. Once on the ship, you refused to walk and stayed in your father's arms. When put down onto the floor, you limped along. Not knowing what was wrong with you, we took off your boot and found that wooden deer. Your father and many of his friends laughed. Silly child, why didn't you tell us?"

Mother burst into laughter; I bent over my mother's knees and laughed, ashamed of myself. As I recall it now, both her interrogation and my feeling ashamed were entirely groundless. It was pointless to mention something that had happened over ten years before and treated it as if it had just happened. However, at that time, there was endless love and innocence between the two of us.

"What you feared most was when I fixed my eyes. I don't know why feared it even today. Whenever I gazed out of the window or looked blank for a moment, you would come to call me and shake me. You would ask, 'Mom, why aren't your eyes moving?' Sometimes, when I wanted you to come to hug me, I would deliberately keep still and gaze somewhere."

I myself have no idea why I behaved that way. Perhaps it was because I wanted to interrupt her train of thought, for my mother was often in a bad mood when she fixed her eyes. Anyway, it remains a mystery.

"But you also love to gaze somewhere. While you were having meals, you would look blankly at the scripts and paintings on the walls and the clock and vase on the table. A meal would take a couple of hours, as if you had been counting the rice grains in your bowl one by one. I grew impatient and removed all those things."

I still remember this, very clearly. I am still in the habit of sitting alone in deep contemplation.

As she said all these things, I would beam broadly, but my eyes would be filled with tears. When she finished, I would wipe my

eyes with her sleeves and bend over her knees motionless. At that moment, the universe had disappeared; there were only my mother and me. In the end, I also disappeared; only my mother remained — for I was originally a part of her!

What a pleasant surprise it was to come to discover and complete myself based on what my mother had said about me! She knew me and loved me from the beginning. She had taken to me even when I had not realized or admitted that I existed in the world. It was not until three years old that I came to find myself, love myself, and know myself. Nevertheless, the self I know is but one hundredth — indeed, one ten-millionth — of that in my mother's mind.

Little friends, when you have found someone in the world who know you and love you thousands of times more than you do, won't it move you to tears? Won't you love her whole-heartedly? Won't you allow her to love you whole-heartedly?

One day, I went up to my mother, raised

my head, and asked her, "Mom, why do you love me?" She put down the needlework, put her cheeks against my forehead, and said softly, yet without hesitation, "There's no other reason — because you are my daughter!"

Little friends, I don't believe there is a second person in the world who can say that. "There's no other reason." How resolute and how irreversible these words sounded when spoken by my mother! She does not love me because I am called "Bing Xin" or any other artificial appellation. Her love is unconditioned; the only reason is that I am her daughter. In a word, her love brushes aside everything, sweeps away everything, and dusts off, layer by layer, all that surrounds me which makes what I am now — its object is my self.

If I go behind the curtain, change the history of my life and everything else in the past twenty years, and get back on stage again — even if no one else in the world recognizes me — my mother, as long as I remain her daughter, will embrace me with her steadfast, endless love. She loves my body, she loves my soul, she loves everything in front of me, behind me, on my left, on my right, everything of my past, my future, and my present.

The stars in the sky are falling into the ocean like showers of rain, giving off a constant whistling sound. Mountainous waves are surging up, all the buildings on the earth are spinning, and the sky is rolling up like a piece of blue paper. Tree leaves are dancing in the air, birds have flown back to their nests, and beasts are hiding in their caves. In this pandemonium, as long as I can find her and throw myself into her arms... Everything in the world believes in her. Her love for me does not change with the destruction of everything.

Her love embraces not only me, but all those who love me; and as she loves me, she loves all children and all mothers in the world. Little friends, let me tell you a remark which is quite plain to children but which is considered deeply profound by adults: "The world was created in this way!"

No two things in the world are identical (even two hairs on your head can't be of the same length); however, the love of mothers all over the world (Little friends, let's sing the praises of it together!) — whether concealed or apparent, showing or hidden, whether measured by the bushel, by the ruler, or by the mind, whether it is my mother's love for me, your mother's for you, or his or her mother's for him or her — is exactly the same. Little friends, I dare to say and dare to believe that, throughout the ages, no one has had the guts to refute my claim. When I discovered this sacred secret, I was so joyous and so moved that I bent over my desk and cried bitterly.

The upsurge of my emotions has reached its culmination, which, I know, is not good for my health. Besides, I know what I have just written is not outside the scope of your wisdom. Outside the window, the autumn rain is coming down, now heavily now slightly, and the fragrance of roses is praising in silence the love of their Mother Nature.

As my mother is not here — but I know her love has always been with me, and she said so, too — I have no way, for now, of inquiring about my childhood; anyway, I will write to my mother. I will say, "Dear Mother, please note down anything about me that I don't know yet as soon as it occurs to you and then mail it to me. Now, I am sort of an archaeologist who is going to study the mysterious self, based on the information provided by you, who knows me perfectly well."

You are blessed by God, little friends! You are in your mothers' arms! Little friends, tell you what, when you finish reading this letter, put down the newspaper and go to find your mother at once — if she is not home, sit on the threshold and wait for her quietly — whether in the room or in the yard. Find her, embrace her, kiss her on both cheeks, and say, "Mother! If you have time, please tell me stories about my childhood." When she sits down, you climb on her knees, lean against her breast — you can hear the slow pulse of her heart — raise your head, and you will hear innumerable wonderful stories about you, stories you have never heard of before, sung out from your mother's mouth like heavenly music.

Then, little friends, I would like you to tell me what she has told you.

Now that I am ill and my mother is not here, you must be feeling very sorry for me; however, I can't thank you enough. When the Creator delivered me to my mother, He endowed me with the gift of memory; now He delivers me from heavy coursework and sets aside seven days and nights for me to recall my mother's love. Thanks to these remembrances, every minute of my illness is sweet.

Little friends, see you next time. Please remember me to your mothers!

Your friend,

Bing Xin

Letter 13

January 10th. Night

Dear Mother,

I don't know how you would feel when you read this. I remember that you have a daughter who, during the twenty years she spent with her mother, brought the latter both laughter and annoyance. Six months ago, she went across the ocean. Then, she was taken ill and stayed at Sharon. This letter is written by her.

Now, she is under a solitary lamp. From downstairs came the sound of plaintive but mellifluous music and the laughter of many girls by the railings. Yet, she is not going out. She has just replied a few letters from friends in China. Suddenly, her emotion is thrown into turmoil. This is the first time that she has been profoundly affected since she came to Sharon. When asked "How is your study?" and "Did you go to Washington D.C. and New York at Christmas?" she does not know how to respond. Time flies past her eyes; she has got nowhere but is amusing herself with illness.

She does not know to whom she should entrust her entangled heart for consolation. She has scribbled on a scrap of paper, with her weak wrist, "Perhaps that is still no comparison to partings in the world" for countless times. She is writing away until she suddenly realizes that there is no space left on the scrap of paper, and she has no idea how that sentence has come into her mind.

Oh, Mother! I shouldn't have said that, for in my life there is only flower, and light, and love; in my life there is only blessing, there is no curse. But I can't help feeling gloomy occasionally. The occasional sad yet calm thoughts have become almost unbearable to me, who has always lived in blessings. Behold! The little boat is tossed around in raging billows. The boatman, totally at a loss, is holding on to the mast and crying out in pain the name of the benevolent "Heavenly Empress." When the boat of my heart is tossed this way and that in the bottomless sea of my thoughts, the moment I write down the word "mother" — even though you are tens of thousands of miles away, Mother — my masterless heart comes safely to land.

Letter 14

January 15th, 1924. Night

My little friends,

Having woken up from my afternoon nap, I sauntered into the western cloister and saw a sick girl. I was talking to her by her bed when I looked up and saw a lone star shining brightly on the tip of a pine. The girl said, "This is the first star you see tonight, why not make a wish?" — Meanwhile, she began to hum a tune, which is as follows:

Star light

Star bright
First star I see tonight
Wish I may
Wish I might
Have the wish I wish tonight

Little friends, this is a most melodious rhyme, but I don't want to translate it. For the value of a nursery rhyme is in its formal features; if we translate it into Chinese, its aural appeal will be lost. The general meaning of the song is simply her remarks to me. (If you can read it yourself, or if your sister, brother, aunt or mother can teach you to read it, that would be better.) On hearing her words, without hesitation, I folded my palms and said toward heaven, "I hope my mother does not worry too much about me, who is safe and happy, though tens of thousands of miles away."

I calculate that, by today or tomorrow, my mother will have received my letter about me being ill and taken to hospital in the hills. I can't possibly know how they will discuss the matter and worry about me. In

fact, being carefree, I am enjoying a tranquil life here.

In the letter I mailed to one of my friends at home on December 19th last year, I wrote, "Sharon Infirmary is as cold as an icy hole. And I am exposed to the biting wind all day. Sitting by the fire, you certainly won't think of the one who is struggling with Nature in a world of ice and snow." These words now seem too resentful and senseless; such a gentle struggle is unheard of.

Birth, aging, illness, and death are important and inevitable matters in one's life. No matter how noble or how great a person is, he simply can do nothing about those things which are of immediate concern to himself. What he can do is to treat himself as an onlooker and let Nature have his own way. Little friends, I can't help extolling his deliberation and subtlety when I watch Nature arrange my fate with his nimble fingers.

I used to pass by Lake Waban several times a day. I would think about my assignments while enjoying the glow of the sunset.

Occasionally, I would spare some time to go boating. Now looking at the bright ripples, now glancing at my watch on which the second hand was ticking away, I felt utterly miserable. However, it was quite absurd to do nothing but admire the beauty of Nature all day. The omniscient Creator, seeing what my trouble was, hit upon an idea and bestowed on me an illness that could be cured only by casting aside everything and sailing on the sea of Nature.

How about me now? I am living a life of flowers, being exposed to the bright sun, gentle breeze, and light drizzle; I am living a life of birds, flying among hill tops and at the waterside and resting in a nest surrounded by air; I am living a life of water, running away; I am living a life of clouds, rolling and drifting at will. I will no longer read dozens or even hundreds of remarkable poems and poetry talks at one go as routine assignments — no more act of stupidity like that. Now, I will take up a poem, even if as short as four or six lines long, recite it repeatedly, and think it over and over.

I have always loved the sound of fine snow and light rain and the sight of a bright moon and stars. In the past, my heart was occupied by all kinds of worldly defilements. On occasion, when something caught my eye or ear, I would bring my heart back immediately and never once did I let it have its own way. What about now? Now, my heart — I don't know how to describe it — is like a moth breaking through the cocoon, or a hawk soaring in the skies...

Fine snow and light rain on the eaves and the bright moon and stars at the railings — all these are near at hand now. Besides, they are supposed to be my second life in my illness. Before I was ill, they couldn't be my second life even if I would like it.

There is something even better about this story. "You should walk a few miles on the hill every day." At these words from the amusing doctor, I simply couldn't compliment him enough. Little friends, those words initiated my roaming life!

Behind the hill is a forest, through which

a narrow path zigzags among the sunlit trees until it vanishes into the distance. I walked along the path as far as where a boulder lay. Overlooking the hills from the top of the boulder, I could see pines far and near, high and low. Whenever I want to indulge myself in some fanciful or sobering thoughts, I will take that path. Strolling alone, with head bent down, I heard dry leaves and dead branches chattering away on top of the trees. Beneath my feet, the thin frost on the grass rustled. At that moment, amidst the shadows of trees, I was lost in thought, as if I felt sad about something.

In front of the hill are wide open fields, layer upon layer, extremely large, bathed in the morning sunshine. At the far end of the fields is a huge frozen lake, surrounded by small hills and tall trees. Local children love to go skating here. What I enjoy doing most is to walk as fast as I can across the lake. Whenever I need revitalization, I will take this path. Bathed in the warm sunshine, I sat under a tree, surveying the boundless, glittering silver sea. How vast heaven and earth are, and how tiny human beings are, I thought. When, on my way back, I slid across the frozen lake, hearing the cool breeze sweep past my ears, I felt joyful yet detached, as if something had dawned upon me.

One summer day three years ago, I wrote a short piece during my stay in the Western Hills in Beijing. I can't remember it clearly now. Roughly, it is like this:

Only in deep valleys in the morning
Can we converse with Nature.
The plan is made,
Rocks nod,
Plants smile.
Creator!
On our hasty night journey
Ahead of us,
Arrange a few more
Deep valleys in the morning!

As it turns out, the few deep valleys in the morning that the Creator has arranged for me are located in Sharon, tens of thousands of miles away from Beijing. How "careless" I am, and how "willing" the Creator! I also remember "sound of footsteps in a deserted valley," and one of Du Fu's poems which begins with "Lovely lady, fairest of the time, / Hiding away in an empty valley." Have you read it before, little friends? I have tried again and again to recite it, but I can only

remember the following eight lines:

Lovely lady, fairest of the time,
Hiding away in an empty valley;
She says she comes from a good family,
But has fallen to the grass roots
....
The lady picks a flower but does not put
  it in her hair,
Gathers cypress leaves, sometimes a
  handful.
In the cold air her thin green sleeves are
  wavy;
At dusk she stands leaning by slender, tall
  bamboos.

At dusk, I went there again and this time
  I remembered:
Where, before me, are the ages that have
  gone?
And where, behind me, are the coming
  generations?
I think of heaven and earth, without limit,
  without end,

And I am all alone and my tears fall down.

On my way back, I recited this:

The careless clouds issue from behind the peaks,
And birds, tired of flying, think of coming home.
As the veiled sun is going down west,
I tarry to fondle the lonely pine.
Little friends, I hope you study ancient authors diligently, because more often than not they have already said what you want to say in a certain situation.

Spring is smiling behind the clouds. When it comes, I have more pleasant news for you. I walk farther each day and have discovered a few places where there are broken bridges and streams. Try to imagine this: without any sorrow or anxiety, one wanders around, trying to draw back the curtains that hide Nature from view and then tiptoe into the celestial palace...

Little friends, please feel grateful for such illness and such a life. In my life there are only blessings, no curses.

It is time to go to bed. I am going to lie down and look at stars. Little friends, I bless you with the warmest heart.

Yours in Sharon,
Bing Xin

P.S. On the four sides of the spacious hall hang green curtains. In one corner, a few girls are murmuring and chuckling on the bench by the window. In another, the gramophone is playing soft, melodious violin music. I am writing this letter at the square table in the middle of the hall. A girl is sitting opposite me and doing my portrait. Now and then, she asks me to raise my head to look at her. I now listen to the music and the low voices, now feel the flow of emotions, and now pause and think. When it is done, I read the letter through and find it is disjointed and lacks organization. Nevertheless, it is an authentic record of the course of the babbling brook that is my heart. I therefore will not reorganize the letter but will mail it this evening.

Letter 15

Sharon
February 4th, 1924

Benevolent little friends,

If there is any room in your unbounded loving heart, I would like to introduce a few lovable girls to you. I hope you hold them dear.

M's room is next to mine. She is an innocent girl, but she suffers from serious neurosis. A mild shock or some joy will affect her severely. She has been in bed for four and a half years, but her condition hasn't changed much. Sometimes, just as she is feeling a little better, at night her temperature rises again. Having read the thermometer, she will bury her face in the pillow and whimper. She has a very happy family, but she has to be quarantined because of illness. My childlike innocence was

awakened entirely by her. She often sits on her
bed and mutter to herself, "My father loves
me, my mother loves me, I love..." I will listen
attentively to what she is going to say next.
Then, she continues, "I love myself." I burst out
laughing, and so does she. This tender, naïve,
yet miserable girl has won the affection of
many of the female patients here.

R's room is next to M's. She is loved
by everyone, and she loves everyone. She
certainly has very deft fingers, for she can
make many ingenious and interesting objects
with a needle or a pen. These days, she is
learning Chinese characters with me. On
the first day, I taught her tian (heaven),
di (earth), and ren (man). She said, "You
Chinese are so metaphysical. You learn such
lofty characters as beginners? We only learn
words like "cat" and "dog." I laughed, yet
I thought what she said was sensible. She
is a quick learner; she speaks clearly, and
the characters she writes are pretty square
and upright. Apart from these, it is she who
reads the thermometer in the hospital, it is

she who plays the piano every Sunday, it is she who takes care of the newspapers the patients read, and she is in charge of the key to the library. She wears neck-length hair and favors spontaneity; she has been in hospital for six months.

E is only eighteen years old, and yesterday was her birthday. She has no parents; she only has an elder brother. Nineteen months ago, she was taken here, very ill. Now she is somewhat better, but still very weak. She loves to call people "Mother" or "Sister." She yearns for affection and sympathy, but she refrains from showing it and often tries her best to be happy and active though in solitude. However, every time after she has had an injection, I can see her, through the half-open door, burying her head in the pillow and weeping silently. She is in her prime, yet what a life she is leading!

D is an Irish girl. She often inquires after my family, especially my father; I used to respond casually. Later, I heard that her father was an alcoholic and used to abuse his children when drunk. Her life at home was miserable. In order to keep away from her father, she moved to her grandmother's house and when she heard people talk of parental love, she would shed tears. Yesterday, she was with me when I received a letter from home. She asked, half enviously and half gloomily, "Is the letter from your father? How thick it is!" Fortunately, she knows no Chinese. I replied at once, "No, it's from my mother. My father is very busy and seldom writes to me." She blushed and smiled, but she also seemed to be relieved. In fact, to each letter from home,

my father, mother, and younger brothers respectively contribute a few sheets. I believe the greatest misfortune in one's life is falling out of the love of one's parents. I don't want to close my eyes and imagine it, nor do I dare to. Poor girl! She is suffering not only from physical illness but from mental trauma.

A stays in a small building at the back of the hospital. I didn't notice her until one day I turned my head unintentionally in the dining room and saw her smiling at me. She had very long eyelashes, and I could see elegance and gentility in her eyes — definitely not typical of the Westerners. Outside of the dining room, I learned of her name and address. That night, we talked for half an hour in her building, and I was surprised at her shyness and meekness. When we were discussing seascape, she gave me a picture with a lighthouse in it, much to my surprise. She has been here for nearly two years, but they tell me there is little sign of improvement

in her. She lies in a small corridor all day, in front of which there is a winding path and a forest and at the back of which is a small bridge over the flowing stream. She told me that whenever there was a storm, she would, looking at the desolate landscape, think of "life" and grow agitated and unhappy. I comforted her, and she thanked me, yet both our faces were bathed in tears.

Certainly, people who are suffering are not limited to these few individuals. Due to my limited energy, however, I cannot provide more examples here.

This morning, I woke up at dawn. Under the faint light of the morning star, in the midst of thousands of pines shrouded in mist, I put on my coat and sat on the bed. Looking down the corridor, I saw short beds placed end to end, white pillows, and girls tossing in their dreams. Suddenly, I felt a deep pang of sorrow. Why should there be love in life if it is not meant for these people? These miserable souls need infinite concern and sympathy. As an individual person, I am insignificant; apart from praying to Heaven, I can only seek help from you, my pure, great little friends who are tens of thousands of miles away.

Little friends, because of my correspondence with you, I have been rebuked by many friends of mine. They disapprove of my providing you only with sad thoughts. Children are not supposed to read this kind of stuff too often, nor should I write this kind of stuff too often. For the sake of the spiritual delight and peacefulness on the part of both you and me, I am ashamed of and thankful for their admonition. However, life is not always hilariously happy; illness and separation are acid fruits of happiness. In the quiet sadness there is infinite solemnity. It is an essential part of a great life. Fan Zhongyan said, "Be the first to become concerned with the world's troubles." The Buddha said, "Let me be the one to go down into the hell." Besides, it is an element in one's life that one will know sooner or later, whether by hearing, seeing, or experiencing. What's the point, then, of concealing it from my dear little friends? It is not too inappropriate, I think, for me to share with you what I have happened to experience over the past six months.

I fare much better than them. In the first place, I have a happy family, which nips gloomy thoughts in the bud. Unlike them, who are bedridden and have to face listlessly the same part of a hill all day, I am able to walk around in the hills. I am a visitor anyway; it's the same staying in the college or in the hills. Certainly I will feel delighted if someone comes to see me but, if no one comes, I won't be particularly disappointed or sad. Their homes, however, are close at hand but they have to stay away from their parents and beloved ones because of illness. When bad weather makes it hard for their family members to come to see them, they tend to be stricken with grief. Month after month, year after year, they are immersed in pain and resentment. Such is their life.

It is not too hard to infer that those who are suffering and those who are in need in the world are certainly not confined to such a small place as Sharon. Little friends, you may have seen more instances than I have. Whose responsibility it is to come to their help and console them? If we are indifferent to them, what is the use of the passionate love that Heaven has given us?

So, little friends, what we can contribute is no more than a flower, a picture, a few comforting words, a solicitous visit, or even a pitiful glance. To us, it is not too much effort, but to the sick, who are leading a miserable and monotonous life, it is as good as a gift from Heaven. When the visit is over, when the flower has withered, and when we have forgotten all this, they, lying on their sickbed, are still thinking of you and are full of gratitude.

Needless to say, I have received several gifts from little friends during my illness. Out of your complete and passionate love, a short letter or a small gift does wonders. Little friends, I cannot express my gratitude in words; what I can do is to fold my palms in praise of your purity and greatness.

The persons I beg you to keep in mind are abroad but, when you think of those poor children, you might be able, by judging another person's feelings by your own, to show solicitude for the sick ones around you. Little friends, don't suppose it is useless to be concerned for someone who is tens of thousands of miles away. "Feed your soul on great thoughts!" Compassion, which will help you embark on great enterprises in the future, originates from miscellaneous instances of pity and tenderness.

Writing this letter in the windy and snowy corridor, not only are my hands cold, but my train of thought freezes. For no reason, I opened a letter from a Chinese friend in Boston, which sent me sighing with great sorrow. She has reminded me that today is New Year's Eve on the Chinese calendar! There must be incessant cheers and laughter among red lanterns and green wine; here, there is nothing but silent hills in whirling snow... I don't want to continue writing. I wish you a most Happy New Year!

Your faithful and passionate friend,
Bing Xin

Letter 16

Sharon, the Blue Hills
March 1st, 1924

Bing Shu, my dear brother,
It's wonderfully comforting to receive two lengthy and sincere letters from you. Yes, indeed! "The sun's rays that filter through the pines are the messenger who brings greetings from your younger brother; the cool wind at night is the consoling words of siblings." Good brother! I love and appreciate the poetic and comforting words of yours.

Much to my surprise, I also received the Selection of Famous Ci Poetry through the Ages. I love it immensely. Father said perhaps I already had a copy. I have a Selection of Ci Poems of Ancient and Modern Times, which is now on the bookshelf in Beebe Hall. How nasty it is that, whenever I ask for Chinese books, they will use any excuse to prevent me, as if every Chinese book were full of abstruse philosophy and would kill all my brain cells.

Not wanting to act against their good intentions, I persuade myself to be content with the short poems I have brought from the hospital. Yesterday evening when I received the collection, I read it page by page as a cherished possession, and I thought I was very lucky to have a little brother who understood me so well.

The style of these poems seems a bit too refined, and misprints are not rare. But in general, it is a quite good collection.

You asked me where I can find more poetic places, at home or abroad. Now I tell you without hesitation, "Abroad, of course!"

First of all, when in Beijing, you can't be with lakes and hills day and night; second, a traveler in a foreign country, with his or her particular feelings, seems to be able to appreciate poetry better.

Having left the shore of Huangpu River, being alone on a ship in the Pacific, surrounded by the azure sky and the blue sea, I often remembered these two lines: "They wandered by the fathomless waters of the deep. / All the world tells the tale of their misery." For I accidentally found that the people on the ship, when leaning over the railings and looking down at the waves breaking over the bows, seemed to have a touch of sadness on their faces.

In Wellesley, Lake Waban was my sole companion. I went there every day, sometimes walking on the shore and sometimes sailing on the lake. On the day before Mother's birthday, I went there again. By the lake, I became homesick and suddenly remembered Zuo Fu's ci poem to the tune of "Waves Dredging Sand":

Tender waters, soft sound of the oars,
Fragrant green grass on the islets;
A few peach trees half hide the red mansion.
This is the spirit of spring hills
Summoned into the solitary boat.

Homesick dreams have not ended,
Why do I bother about idle melancholy?
Zhongzhou left behind, I am passing Fuzhou:
Throw it into the river so it can drift out to sea,
Don't turn round again!

Finding that both the scenery and the emotions were quite similar, I picked up a stone by the lake, inscribed on it with a knife these two lines: "Homesick dreams have not ended, / Why do I bother about idle melancholy?" I threw the stone as far as I could into the lake and, without looking back, I walked away. From that day on, that stone will, I believe, lie in the bottom of the lake till the end of the world. As long as the lake doesn't run dry and the stone doesn't rot, my nostalgia, symbolized by the stone, will be indestructible forever.

The houses of American people, except those in urban areas, are usually built next to a hill or a stream. Quite dainty are the houses, and flowers are planted randomly outside the windows or beside the fence, which easily reminds one of the line "Here every household has their doors shielded by the green." As there is no enclosing wall, a typical American house is, though spacious enough, lacking in depth. A passerby can see green sleeves and red clothes through the window and hear the sounds of chatting, laughing, and piano playing. "The deep court has come well under sunset's gleams." "How deep is the inner garden that is deep?" "Deep in a dark corner I dwell." "Within the wall there is a swing, without, a path." "The Milky Way is a red wall, separating those on either side completely." — All these lines from ci poems are irrelevant here.

Between stretches of open country, there are thick woods; the paths wind along the undulating hills as if they are part of Nature.

It must be more beautiful when the country is covered with wild flowers in the spring. However, as you travel across the hills, you can't find a single Buddhist monastery surrounded by walls. "A winding path leads to a calm retreat, / And deep the greenery round the chamber for meditation." "From the monastery come the faint Buddhist chants, / The moon hides behind the high walls and time lapses." "One lone township lies among towering mountain ranges." "Having drowned my sorrows, I slept on the city wall." "At twilight rises wisps of smoke from an isolated town that is shutting its gate." "Curtain raised, stars sparse, the courtyard is quiet, / From the guarded town come the faint tolls of night-hour gongs." — These lines, again, are meaningless here.

In brief, everything here reminds you of the New World, and you can find signs of the beginning of the world everywhere. In our country, there is an atmosphere of antiquity and solemnity. The city walls and palaces are in ruins now, but when you see them, you can't help but feel "Raising my head, I desire to make their acquaintance; lowering it, I feel like falling on my knees." My dear venerable, five-thousand-year-old homeland!

I remember I went south last summer. One morning, the train was passing Suzhou; it went along the city walls for miles. Heavy mists hung over the city, a few small boats were anchored in the moat, and the higher stories of a pagoda was visible on top of the walls — they made a beautiful picture. At that time, I had already known that once I left my country, I would never see such scenery again.

As to life in the hills, apart from reading, sightseeing, and chatting with girl friends, I have nothing to do in the daytime. The poems of Xie Lingyun, one of my favorite poets, have described my life here perfectly, and there is no need for me to add one more word:

Lying in bed because of illness, I refuse to meet visitors;
I abandon the crowds and walk amid a

cloudy fog from peak to peak.
With precipices and ravines before my eyes,
I miss my brothers who are far away.

And:

During my stay in the capital city,
I never gave up going sightseeing among
  hills.
Now that I've returned to a natural surrounding,
I isolate myself from the world.
....
Being ill in bed, I have abundant time.
Sometimes, I practice calligraphy,
And hold a book in hand;
At mealtimes and before going to bed, I
  tell some jokes.
....
It is impossible to have the best of both worlds,
But perhaps I can arrive at a full understanding
  of life.
And suddenly I recall "Recalling home,
I pace the moonlight, stand in the clear
evening; / Thinking of younger brothers,

watching clouds, at midday half asleep" by Du Fu, and "It's not bad that illness brings me leisure, / There's no better medicine than feeling at ease" by Su Dongpo. These lines describe exactly what my life is like at present. The Blue Hill is covered in pine trees, and there is snow everywhere. In the moonlight, everything looks beautiful beyond description. After supper, I'm in the habit of standing in front of the building for a while, and in the chilliness I will naturally think of my home. From 3 p.m. to 5 p.m. every afternoon, it's the time for rest, but how can I fall asleep in the daytime? So, I lie awake on my bed and look at the clouds in the sky. Sometimes, I take out the letters from home and read them again, and naturally I will think of my younger brothers. Your brother Bing Zhong was afraid that I wouldn't be able to write often. He didn't know that, as I have more leisure time and a more peaceful mind during illness, I can write more letters than usual. Besides, since I was ill, I haven't taken any medicine — "There's no better medicine than feeling at ease." How true it is!

One good thing about reading many ancient poems is that they help to make my writing more economical. On the one hand, I'm happy to be able to sympathize with these ancient poets; on the other hand, "how I regret that I couldn't go back to ancient times and say what ancient people wanted to say before them." I have said too much. Owing to your selection of ci poems, I have larded my letter with quotations. Ha! Who's to blame, then?

The Blue Hill can be absolutely stunning sometimes. On Feb. 7th, that is, following five days' snow storm, all the trees were shrouded in a crust of ice. As the brilliant sun rose in the east and shone on the silver trees, the light reflecting off them was dazzling. I went downstairs and took a brief walk in the snowy wood. Casually looking back, I found I had wended my way through a bush of ice and jade, and in one corner of the small building, the curtains of my room were barely visible. Although, generally speaking, those "icy heights" are unbearably cold, these "crystal towers and courts of jade" were on earth rather than on high.

On the morning of the 9th, I went out with a girl friend on a sled. Pulled by two galloping horses, we traveled around the Blue Hill. As we passed through the thick woods on our way, the icy branches flicked our clothes and produced a loud and clear sound. The earth was all white. What a pure, untainted world! The most beautiful scene was ice beads hanging on the branches of wild cherries, red alternating with white, sparkling in the sunlight. No jewelry was more resplendent than this.

On the way, my friend pointed to the green hills undulating on the horizon. It suddenly dawned on me that I was really far away from home, for "the distant green hills" were no longer those on the Central Plains of China. At that time, my thoughts turned to things distant. Brother! I have always considered "truth" to be the sole criterion for good writing, but now I figure that not only is my writing before I went abroad not true, but what I wrote thereafter is not entirely true.

It's my firm belief that, whether it is a human feeling or scenery that you are trying to describe, when at its farthest end, it can't, whatsoever, be expressed in words. Even if you have made several attempts to write or say something, you simply can't find the apt words to describe that feeling or scenery and, in the end, you have to put down your pen or remain silent. In order to retain at least some impression of such scenes, you have no alternative but to write down a few descriptive words. Or even better, you can just scribble some lines on the paper, as in primitive times people kept records by tying knots. If, some day in the future, you can recollect something of the past by looking at these hardly discernible black marks again, you should be more than satisfied.

Before I went abroad, I wrote more than my emotions required it. After, my emotions are more than I can write about. There are many exquisite scenes here which can be turned into words, but more often than not I can't bring myself to produce anything. As Xin Qiji said in one of his ci poems to the tune of "Fascinating Luo Fu":

As a lad I never knew the taste of sorrow,
But loved to climb towers,
Loved to climb towers,
And drag sorrow into each new song I sang.
Now I know well the taste of sorrow,
It is on the tip of my tongue,
On the tip of my tongue,
But instead I say, "What a fine, cool autumn
    day!"

This poem made me utterly despondent.

Though he only mentions "sorrow," it actually encompasses all other feelings. I wonder if I'm the only person who is tormented by the fact that words and feelings don't correspond to each other, or if everyone is so.

As a Beijing proverb goes, "On the 15th day of the 8th lunar month clouds obscure the moon; on the 15th day of the first lunar month snow falls on the lanterns." On the Mid-Autumn Day last year, the moon was invisible here; the night before, the moon shone brightly in the sky. I was thinking that the Chinese proverb might not apply to Western climate when, on the night of the Lantern Festival, it began to snow. After the 18th day of the first lunar month, I could see the moon every night when I woke up. On the moonlit pillow, dreams and the moon succeeded each other. It was even better on the last two nights. When I woke up it was approaching daybreak. A golden crescent moon was in the dark blue sky, and facing the concave of the crescent, not far away, was a big star. In the cloudless sky there was only one star and one moon — what a marvelous picture!

How about you all on the night of the Lantern Festival? I heard that, on the evening of the 24th day of the twelfth lunar month, Mother missed me at the family feast, and you, my brothers, told jokes to comfort her. Indeed, the weed has grown into a walking stick! I was just joking. Many thanks for that.

The sheet is full and I'll just stop here. I think it would be good if you could let our little friends read this.

Bing Xin

Letter 18

Little friends,

Good to see you again, my dear little friends! I haven't written to you for many days, but that is not my real intention. You know, the letters I mailed to China were sometimes delayed or lost. Besides, though I

could write as regularly as before during my illness, you might not bother to read every one of my letters. What's more, my doctors told me to get as much rest as possible. So I rested.

Since I began writing to you, I have been either ill or busy. Now that I have recovered and haven't got busy yet, I feel it necessary to write a long letter to catch up on many things that had happened.

Would you like me to begin from last year? I know little friends are never tired of listening to past events. However, I can't give a lot of details; I can only give a general outline of it as far as I can remember. My purpose is to fill the gap; otherwise, you must think it too abrupt that I flew from Kobe to Wellesley overnight.

Kobe; August 20th, 1923

In the morning, I went ashore with many people and saw from afar the gigantic anchor, which was formed by the grass grown there. It rested halfway up the Anchor Hill, attractively green.

The streets in Kobe are quite similar to those in China, except that the stores along the streets are lower. Various kinds of fancy toys and children books were displayed in the showcases, around which gathered many children. The clothes of Japanese children are more colorful and attractive than ours. The children looked very lovely with their plump faces, jet-black eyes, and thick black hair.

There were a few houses at the foot of the hill. The walls were made of wood, and the windows, bamboo. Flowers of different colors reached over the walls, and outside the walls there was a small bridge, beneath which a stream was flowing. The whole atmosphere was tranquil and elegant. We had planned to go up to see the male and female gorges (two waterfalls), but while we were walking up we came across some fellow passengers who were rushing down. They said it was about time. For fear that the ship sailed away without us, we had to turn back.

When ashore, we all went to the post office to buy stamps and mail letters. The Kobe Post Office was crowded with Chinese students. The inseverable parting sorrows! Having been away from home for only three days, do they have so much to say to their family and friends?

When we were back on the ship, someone said jokingly, "What's the use of vernacular Chinese? We and the Japanese speak different languages, and not every Japanese knows English. Write then. 'What's the busiest place?' They looked at me not knowing what to say. 'Where is the bustling downtown area?' They understood immediately and directed us to the busiest part of the town." I couldn't help laughing.

Yokohama; August 21st

At dusk we were nearing Yokohama. The setting sun, covered by white clouds, took on a bright red, like a Japanese red-paper lantern — a matter of association.

The rolling hills looked great, even from the railings over which I was leaning. Then, I threw a few sealed tin containers for roll film into the sea, in which I had put a few slips of paper, and let them drift away. On the slips I had written:

No matter which fisherman picks this up, I wish you good luck. With the sincerity of an Oriental, I pray to God to bless you, fisherman on the oriental waters. And verse lines such as "I long to fly back on the wind, yet dread those crystal towers, those courts of jade, freezing to death among those icy heights!"

Yokohama was only a transfer station, for we took a tramcar there to Tokyo. First, we visited the Chinese Youth Association, and then we went into a Japanese restaurant to enjoy Japanese cuisine. That restaurant was called "Celestial Fragrance," or something like that. Customers had to take off their shoes before entering the restaurant. I was definitely not used to that, and we all laughed. The waitresses were bare-footed. They didn't understand what we said, so we could only smile at each other. Sitting on the floor, I looked up and found that the walls and windows were all made of wooden boards, as smooth as if they had just been wiped. It was overcast outside the windows; it was a clean and quiet place. Our food was very simple: rice, beef, dried vermicelli, and pickled vegetables. Both the rice and the dishes were hard, and I only ate a little.

It began to pour right after dinner, but we were not going to give up touring, although it made it difficult for us to do so in a leisurely way — we had to stay in our bus, which dashed in the rain from one place to another. We paid very brief visits to places such as Hibiya Park, Yasukuni Shrine, and the National Museum. We went to altogether six or seven places, but apart from going upstairs and downstairs, going in and going out, I couldn't remember anything I had seen. You can't see flowers clearly while riding a horse or in a fog, let alone while riding a bus in the rain. Besides, as I was running a low fever, which got worse because of the rain, I had neither the mental nor the physical strength to look around. Only two places had left a very clear impression on me.

One was the Imperial Palace. A humpback small bridge with white marble balustrades crossed a river, behind which stood the palace walls. I suddenly became clear-headed and went off the bus to take photos. Seeing a policeman coming towards me, I knew he was going to interfere, so I pressed the button quickly before I went back onto the bus. Unfortunately, this shot was ruined by the rain — nothing could be seen on it — but I still kept the film. I heard that the palace was damaged in the earthquake, and I had had the opportunity to have a glimpse of it before the disaster. "A sad stretch of scorched earth."

The other is the Yushukan in Yasukuni Shrine. The trophies from the Sino-Japanese war and the pictures of war on the walls woke up the soldier in me and made my blood boil. Little friends, I am a weak person and can never control my feelings. I don't embrace any doctrine and I am definitely no nationalist. At that moment, however, the blood rushed to my head and made me feel dizzy, and I, in spite of myself, fell to the ground. But even while my fellow travelers were sighing and complaining, I said nothing.

I feel very sorry for telling you this. Although there is a soldier in me, I love Japanese people nevertheless. Humiliation or hatred has no place in my heart, but for the sake of justice, I find myself unable to tolerate such atrocity as human beings oppressing fellow human beings.

Naturally, I love my younger brother, for we are siblings of the same parents. If I have an extra sweet cake and he asks for it, I certainly will give it to him, and smilingly. But if he flaunts his superiority by trying to snatch it away without any explanation, I will, for the sake of justice and with a view to pointing out the right way to him, have to fight back, with tons of affection within me, and won't hesitate to break the cake into bits, if need be.

Please forgive me for speaking so excitedly to you. Let my words circle around for a short while in your minds. I would think twice before I talk like that to someone else. But in you I have absolute trust, for you are capable of the most innocent and holy judgment.

We took the 5 p.m. tramcar and went back onto the ship in Yokohama.

In the sea; after August 24th

Staying on the island of a ship, with nothing but sea water in view, made me feel muddled, and thus unable to give an account of my life on a daily basis. Let me just give a few details.

In the second-class and third-class cabins, there were many Russian refugees, about a hundred of them, whose destination was America. Russians are born musicians. Every night, I stood on the top deck and listened attentively to them playing string instruments down there. Amidst the sound of waves, their music seemed especially plaintive, interwoven with wailing and whispering. These people were also leaving their country. Although different in language, speech, and thinking, we had already exchanged our parting sorrows in the pleasant sensation produced by the plaintive yet lovely music.

The moon was bright that night, and the music playing made me rather reluctant to go back to my cabin. I had a felt blanket draped over my shoulders in hope of resisting the strong sea winds in some measure. The ship sailed on, braving the wind and the waves, and heading for a completely alien land. The sad music seemed to be questioning us what it was for that we had taken the trouble to leave our motherlands and were carrying a ship of parting sorrows. Was it for fame, or for wealth? "I wonder why you part with me so easily; / How many days of reunion are there in a year?" I found I had nothing to say in reply. If it weren't for the sounds of people talking and laughing coming from the top deck which interrupted me, I would probably have stood there throughout the night.

One of us suggested that we collect food and fruit and give them to the refugees' children. Having received quite a lot from Chinese students and other passengers, we took the donations down to the second-class cabin. There were a lot of children among these people. Sometimes, our girls would take some of the little ones upstairs for our amusement — those lovely little kids. But on one occasion, I felt sad and indignant again.

There was a child who was less than two years old and who was the cutest and smartest one. At first, he didn't allow me to

hold him in my arms, and I had a hard time coaxing him with candies, biscuits, and toys that could make noises. When we became familiar, I put him down, and he walked slowly through the soft chairs before he turned back and threw himself onto my knees. We were sporting when I looked up and saw his father standing beside the door of the hall. He was no more than fifty, I figured, but his gray hair and the wrinkles on his face, which bespoke the hardships and misfortunes in his life, made him look like more than sixty. He was gazing at his son; there seemed to be tears in his affectionate eyes. Little friends, tears shed out of true feelings are the most sacred thing in the world, and eyes with sparkling tears are the most solemn and honorable picture. Whenever I see maidens or children with sad or indignant tearful eyes, and women or old people with loving and affectionate tearful eyes, I feel that their teardrops are virtually sending out sacred, awe-inspiring light. Little friends, that is what I revere most. The sight of it tends to make me afraid of raising my head.

This time was no exception. I supported the child in walking, with my head kept low. The nurse of the first-class cabin, whose job was looking after those who were seasick, also caught sight of the Russian beside the door. She looked at him coldly. "Who permitted you to come to the first-class cabin?" she said. "Go down now!"

The poor old man was nervous and reverent. At a loss as to what to do, he forced a smile and picked up his child from my arms. With an apologetic and humiliated look at the nurse, he dragged his tired legs slowly down the stairs.

Who has permitted him to come? No father, if he loves his own child, is willing to leave his beloved son in the care of a stranger — he had come up to look after his son. I had brought the child up, but I couldn't protect his father! All of a sudden, I felt disgruntled. I stared at that obese nurse (not cheerfully, of course), but she

returned a guilty smile. I looked around and found that, although many people had witnessed it, they didn't seem to care at all. I went down. During the supper, I didn't say a word.

The Chinese students on the ship had held two parties. Each time we had asked the ship owner if we could invite these Russians to join us, but he said no on both occasions. These respected Chinese young people didn't believe that money was essential to happiness, and theirs was a saintly motive. Admittedly, the result fell short of expectations, but a world of Great Harmony can only be realized after countless trials and struggles.

The waiters on the Yorkson were all Cantonese, and it must have given them a great joy to see that nine out of ten passengers in the first-class cabin were Chinese young people. What was most praiseworthy was that they were very concerned about what the Americans on the ship were saying about Chinese students. One or two days before the ship arrived at Seattle, they had written a piece aimed at encouraging the Chinese students to bring credit to our nation and posted it up on the deck. Though not smoothly written, it was quite sincere. I only remember one phrase: "we Guangdong guys who have traveled far across the ocean." This refers to their wandering life and the belittlement from westerners. Of course, the Chinese students answered them with an equally earnest letter.

If there was hardly anything to be seen on the sea, the setting sun was interesting enough to gaze at, only it's too hard to describe. I saw flying fish, which had on their backs two wings that resembled those of the locust. I saw two big whales, but their bodies were in the water and I only saw them blowing jets of spray in the distance.

Apart from these, there is not much to be said. We had gatherings, just like those winter conferences and summer conferences, at which we walked about — within the confines of the ship, of course. I attended a few parties and speech gatherings, and the rest of the time I whiled away chatting, looking at the sea, and writing letters.

As we sailed across the Pacific, we gained

an extra day; that is, there were two August 28ths. From then on, the days we spent would be different from those in my native land. When the homesick soul flies to her native land in a homesick dream, the family members are busy going about their work in broad daylight. People who are separated, can't they meet again even in dreams?

Letter 22

The White Mountains
August 6th, 1924

Dear young readers,

Every day at dusk, when I walk alone onto the mountaintop to watch the setting sun, I see the summit of Mount Chocorua. The whole mountain is light green except the peak, which is partly bare and craggy. Perhaps it is too high and too windy for trees to grow up there. On the horizon, the Presidential Range stretches along; Mount

Washington and Mount Madison rise one upon another. I don't know why, but I love Mount Chocorua only.

At dinner, Mrs. C told me that Mount Chocorua was named after an American Indian tribal chief who, because of unrequited love, killed himself by jumping off the peak. But she said that she couldn't remember clearly and that I'd better double-check it by reading books. What a pity it is that such a "heroic" mountain was named after such a sentimental person! Today I took down a book, entitled The White Mountains, from the bookshelf and read through the section on Mount Chocorua. About the death of Chocorua, this book provides a different version from Mrs. C's. I think that story is worth telling to you.

It writes, "Mount Chocorua is probably the most picturesque and beautiful of the mountains of New England." (New England includes six provinces in the eastern U.S.: Maine, NH, Mass., RI, VT, CT. New England, because colonizers from England disembarked here.) "The height of Chocorua is 3,540 ft. On the upper part of the mountain there are brooks; half way up, there are rivers; and at its base, there are lakes. No mountain of New Hampshire has interested our best artists more.

"Chocorua was named after an Indian chieftain who was killed near its summit by white men. The legend was variously narrated, one of which is as follows: When the Indians retreated to Canada, after Lovewell's battle, Chocorua refused to leave the ancient home of his people and the graves of his forefathers. He remained behind, and was friendly to the incoming white settlers, and especially with one Campbell. He had a son, in whom all his hopes and love were centred. On one occasion he was obliged to go to Canada to consult with his people, and, wishing to spare his son the labors of the long journey, he left him with Campbell until his return. The boy was welcomed to the hut of the pioneer and tenderly cared for. One day, however, he found a small bottle of poison, which had been prepared for a mischievous fox, and, with the unsuspecting curiosity of the Indians, he drank a portion of it. Chocorua returned only to find his boy dead and buried. The improbable story of his fatality failed to satisfy the heart-broken chief, and his spirit demanded vengeance. Campbell went home from the fields one day, and saw the dead bodies of his wife and children on the floor of the hut. He tracked Chocorua and found him on the crest of the mountain, and shot him down, while the dying Indian invoked curses on the white men.

"In another version, Chocorua was a prophet of an Indian tribe, and his son was on intimate terms at Campbell's house. The accidental death of the boy, the murder of the family, and the fate of the chief on the mountain-crags follow as in the above story.

"Another account says that Chocorua was a blameless and inoffensive Indian, a friend of the whites, but, during one of the Massachusetts campaigns against the red men, when the Province gave a bounty of £100 for every scalp brought into Boston, a party of hunters pursued the unresisting chieftain and shot him on this mountain, in order to get the bounty-money.

"While dying, the heroic Chocorua opened his eyes wide and cried out, 'A curse upon ye, white men! May the Great Spirit curse ye when he speaks in the clouds, and his words are fire! Chocorua had a son, and ye killed him when the sky was bright! Lightning blast your crops! Winds and fire destroy your dwellings! The Evil Spirit breathe death upon your cattle! Your graves lie in the war-path of the Indian! Panthers howl and wolves fatten over your bones! Chocorua goes to the Great Spirit, his curse stays with the white man!'"

The story stops here. According to the book, "The settlement was afterwards wasted by pestilence, storms, and Indian attacks, and was abandoned by its people. In point of fact, however, the towns in this vicinity were never molested by the Indians. For many years it was impossible to keep cattle, for they sickened and died soon after coming there. The people laid this strange fatality to the operation of Chocorua's curse, until scientists found out that it was due to the presence of lime in the water which they drank.

"The grave of Chocorua is said to be located at the southeast foot of the mountain, but it has not been found yet."

Every day at dusk, I walk alone onto the mountaintop to watch the setting sun, watch it fall from the tip of Mount Chocorua, red as fire! Even the eighteenth-century old houses disappear into the forests. Mountains upon mountains on the earth, there is not a single trace of civilization! At that moment, my spirit tends to wander to hundreds of years ago, imagining that this mountain is now inhabited by the swift red men who decorate their heads with a band and feathers. I feel a little sad. The red men are robust, their complexion a beautiful dark red, quite similar to the Chinese, but they don't value intelligence, and thus are controlled and driven by the white men, and are doomed forever!...

The other day I went to Conway and bought a clay figurine of a red man. He wears a gold crown and a multicolored braid on his head; he wears his long hair loose, in which stand many green feathers; and he wears a belt around his waist. I placed him on my desk and named him Chocorua in memory of my admiration of Chocorua and of my visit to the White Mountains. When the end of the year comes, I plan to arrange for him to visit China and wish my mother a Happy New Year on my behalf. – I've written this in haste.

Yours,
Bing Xin

Letter 23

The White Mountains
August 7th, 1924

Bing Ji, my dear little brother,
It is now in the very early morning; the sun is not yet out and the dew is not yet dry. After breakfast I will have to leave here. I look at the White Mountains with sadness,

but I have to steal this departing morning to drop you a line.

As I saw the Weaving-girl star beside the Milky Way last night, I suddenly remembered that it is the seventh evening of the seventh lunar month in China today. This festival gives rise to innumerable most sweet stories, most sadly moving poems, and occasional recreations. Staying in a strange land, I have long parted with all these things... Well, just leave it alone!

What I want to say is that we really lack recreation. Listless entertainment can't possibly enrich one's life or boost one's career. Recreation is, at least, as valuable as work; or it can be said that recreation is part of work!

Recreation is not entertainment. Behind "entertainment" looms "boredom." In times of sheer boredom, there is entertainment; in times of illness, there is entertainment. When one is disheartened by the national affairs or by life, there is entertainment. Look at the so-called entertainments nowadays; how disorderly they are, and how listless! I'd never take such entertainments for recreation! It is genuine work that gives rise to genuine recreation. In other words, it is those who summon up their energy and devote themselves to genuine work that earnestly long for or are ready for genuine recreation.

Certainly, Chinese people should have Chinese recreation. We have more than four

thousand years of stories, legends, and history. The occasions and justifications for our recreation are twice as many as that of other peoples. Let's begin with the Chinese New Year. After New Year, there is the Lantern Festival. Trees and porches decorated with millions of colorful lanterns — what a splendid picture! And dancing with dragon lanterns is the liveliest game among children. The 3rd of the 3rd lunar month is the festival of Xi in ancient times; it is the best time in a year to go picnicking. Floating wine vessels in a stream is not only an imitation of the ancient customs but also interesting in itself. On the day of Pure Brightness, the 5th of the 24 solar terms, we go to worship at ancestral graves. Though we no longer burn paper money as an offering to the dead, children can be trained to show their ancestors great respect. If the custom of planting trees on the day of Pure Brightness can be put into practice and everyone plants a young tree every year next to the ancestral grave, then, in less than ten years, there will be wooded lands all over China. The 5th day of the 5th lunar month is a festival specially for children. On that day, children are decorated with colorful sachets and threads. It seems that children in the streets and lanes love these few days much more than any other day in a year. It is also the Dragon Boat Festival. It would be fantastic to go boating or have a boating competition between two schools. The 7th day of the 7th lunar month is Daughters' Day — the name itself is lovely enough. In the cool evening, when the wind has dropped, a table is set in the yard, with melons and fruit on it. All the girl friends have been sent for, who chat and laugh in low voices and look up and watch the Herd-boy and the Weaving girl slowly cross the bridge. Children hold a handful of boiled broad beans and give them to each other as gifts; they hold each other's hand, which is called jieyuan ("forming ties"). What a wonderful phrase it is! I have always thought that the meanings of the Chinese character yuan are so subtle that it is extremely hard to translate it; involved in it are the will of Heaven, human feelings, the transmigration through birth and death, and that which is everlasting and unchanging. A poem that Su Shi wrote to his younger brother Su Zhe contains the following lines: "I'd love to be your brother one life after another, to form ties for the ages to come." Little brother, I send these two lines to you as a gift from tens of thousands of miles away!

The 15th of the 8th lunar month is the Mid-autumn Festival. How vivid it is to tell the story about the Toad and the Jade Hare under the silver light of the full moon! The 9th day of the 9th lunar month is the Double Ninth Festival, the day on which people in ancient times climbed mountains and on which we go hiking and visit scenic spots. The National Day, needless to say, must be celebrated, but I find that almost no one celebrates it at home, except for the national flags hung outside administrative buildings and stores.

I won't go into more detail. Open an ancient book, such as Records of Scenery in the Capital City, and you can find many more commemorable days of recreation. I feel Chinese holidays are more refined than those of other countries. Every one of our holidays is associated with gentle, noble stories and strikingly ingenious poems, and even with certain food and equipment at gatherings — such as the dragon boat and the rice dumpling on the 5th of the 5th lunar month, the broad bean on the 7th of the 7th lunar month, the moon cake of the 15th of the 8th lunar month, and innumerable things of all the other festivals and holidays... We don't have to create anything. We only need to call children together; the stories are ready-made, the food is ready-made, the toys are ready-made. When songs are needed for children to sing, there are countless ancient poetry and prose on which new arrangements can be based. Our ancestors have provided us with so many wonderful materials so that we can enjoy the noblest forms of recreation. If we still can't, we are unworthy of their efforts.

It is very good to shatter superstitions;

ing Xin

however, it's a pity that with the shattering of superstitions, these wonderful festivals are increasingly treated with indifference. I'm not advocating superstition, of course. But worshipping idols and children performing stories about immortals are quite different!

I have to stop here. The sun is up now, and the women cooks are preparing breakfast. Before the sun sets this evening, I will be on a small island. And you can guess how much I would love it! My favorite poem in the Book of Poetry is this one:

> The reeds are luxuriant and green,
> The white dew has turned to frost.
> My beloved so dear to me
> Is somewhere beyond the waters.
> ....
> Upriver I search for him,
> He seems to be in the middle of the waters.

I love "the middle of the waters" best, because I find there is something fluttering and hovering about it. Since my journey began, except for a diary and pen and paper, I haven't had any book with me, so there may be some misquotations. Please find them out for me if there is any.

It is estimated that we will be at sea until around the 15th of this lunar month, when the moon becomes full. Now I'm all set, in terms of mood, for the spectacular scene of "a bright moon rising above the sea." If I'm able to produce something interesting about it at that time, I will write to you.

Your sister

Letter 29

Yuan'en Temple

August 31st, 1926

My dearest young readers,

I am home! The word "home" makes me burst into tears of joy and gratitude! Three years abroad, as I recall, has passed in the twinkle of an eye. When I'm writing this letter, my youngest brother Bing Ji is beside me. Outside the window are pink oleanders and green willow branches, against the bright blue sky of Beijing. The scenery of my homeland comes back into my eyes again!

Little friends! If you haven't been away from north China for three years, you won't praise highly its bright blue sky! Get up in the early morning and draw back the curtains, and you will see a wave-like blue sky with one or two masses of pure white cloud drifting slowly, and willow leaves swaying in the morning breeze, sending forth a trace of coolness toward you. You will feel that this kind of faint nostalgia that is "strong in cold, cheerless places" can't possibly be experienced in a foreign land. If you are a person with deep feelings, you will feel something that resembles happiness but is not, or something that resembles melancholy but is not. Stand and gaze for a while, and you probably will shed tears as if you have no one to rely on.

When abroad, I came across such clouds

and such a sky only twice. The first time was a summer day the year before last on the peak of the White Mountains in New Hampshire. I had just woken up from an afternoon nap when I received a letter from a friend in England. It was a letter full of friendly sentiments and nostalgia, a letter describing the scenery in Oxford with dream-like fascination. With mixed feelings of melancholy and joy, I climbed onto the peak with this letter and, all of a sudden, I saw the foreign sky as blue as the ocean! In the midst of the green mountains, this patch of dark blue above permeated all. The setting sun cast its light all over the sky and the earth, purpling the western horizon. The color underwent a myriad of changes in the twinkling of an eye. It turned into silver gray, and then into the whitish color of a fish's belly, and then suddenly into the brightest golden. The mountains were still; however, with the magnificent changes of colors on the horizon, there seemed to be sounds in the heavens! I seemed to have heard the sound

of the sun setting, like waves surging, like
birds chirping, like winds howling. At that
moment, I felt suddenly that my weak heart
was elevated by this mighty impression to
a great height and then, abruptly, pressed
down to the bottom of the sea! Having
perceived the solemnity of Creation, I, with
all my childishness and regardless of the
fact that I had just recovered from illness,
bent over the delicate grass and actually
whimpered away.

The second time was an evening this
spring in Washington D. C. I traveled south
from the dry, cold New York City and found
"spring" in Washington D. C.! A gentle breeze
was blowing, and I took a seat beside the
window. It was in the evening. The hostel of
the National Women's Party was right across
from the white building of the Capitol. My
tired eyes, after a half-day journey, were
awakened by the blue sky behind the building.
Little friends overseas, please forgive me! My
sojourn of two and a half years in the United
States didn't make me think that this was

a stately country until the white building of the Capitol suddenly struck me!

The white building towered in mid-air, like an exquisite palace of the immortals. Illuminated by the powerful lights on the sides of the building, the blue sky behind the building was highlighted. On both sides, also, there were magnificent white marble buildings. In front of the buildings was a very broad white marble street. The snow-white spherical streetlamps were sending out uniform light. The pedestrians were silent among those great edifices. For the first time, I found such a heavenly silence in the United States. At last, I discovered a similarity between Washington D. C. and Beijing!

The homesickness that appeared suddenly was like a raging sea! With a push at the chair, I walked out of this all-quiet high building and headed for the Library of Congress. On the way, I felt unspeakable joy and freedom. The freshly green willow branches were swaying in the evening breeze in early spring. I went into the big reading room as if I had been a frequent visitor, and sat there writing a diary entry. Suddenly, I remembered Lu You's lines: "Being called 'Master', I'm actually a traveler; / Knowing this is not my land, I still make the effort to mount the Tower." Chewing on the meanings of "called" and "make the effort," I began to feel depressed.

I closed the book and strode buoyantly out of the library. Overhead was a star-studded sky. I sighed a deep sigh. I caught sight of a covered pushcart on the roadside. A black man who was selling roasted peanuts and chestnuts was crying out for customers. Since I was taken ill, I had quitted snacks; at that moment, however, I walked up and bought two packs. The swarthy face under the light gave me a gentle smile, which interrupted the homesick dream I had had a hard time securing! Not that I wanted to eat peanuts and chestnuts; I just tried to take Washington D. C. for Beijing!

At this point my wrist becomes weak. Little friends, I feel embarrassed to tell you that, since I came back, I have been ill for over three months. This is the first long letter that I have written since then. I had already been very tired on the journey; on arriving home, I immediately felt relaxed and the demon of disease took advantage of the occasion. I was not a person who easily got ill. I don't know how, but since I started writing to you, I have been either ill or busy. Well, I shouldn't have said so!

Autumn is coming in my native land. Having just recovered, I feel joyous and depressed at once! I have much more to say to you, but let me save it for another day. Luckily, I'm nearer to you now!

I wish you every happiness! I'm your passionate and faithful friend,

Bing Xin

More Letters to Young Readers

Letter 1

Geleshan
December 12th, 1942

Dear little friends,

It is a bright day today, for on this day I resume correspondence with you. The hilltop is bathed in sunshine, and the sun's rays filter through the dense pine forest and become a few misty columns of light. In daylight, a pair of kingfishers skim over the pond and, after singing a few sweet notes, fly into a reddish black bush studded with red beans. Range upon range of green peaks far and near stand steadily and quietly. The Jialing River, like a green brocade belt, meanders towards the east. In the mountain city on the opposite side of the river, innumerable pale white roofs, in a jumbled manner, are half hidden in a thin blanket of fog. All that I see is quite bright, and joyous.

That symbolizes my current state of mind! Twenty years has passed since I first wrote to you in the twelfth year of the Republic of China. In between, I, again with a child's boisterous heart, set out on a life's journey which was filled with color, brightness, and heat. I taught for a period of time and then

became a housewife, and now I am a mother. I have read some more books, got to know some more friends, and traveled to some more places both at home and abroad. In these twenty years, there were no dangerous adventures, nor great pain or ecstasy; however, in my childish heart, I experienced cheerfulness like that of a fine morning, listlessness like that of evening mist, sudden perception like that of Buddhist chanting at midnight, and excitement like that of battle drums and horns at dawn. There are many facts and many feelings that I'd like to share with you, my dear little friends. Please allow me to describe them in detail in the following letters.

Little friends, over the past few years, I have received many letters from you. Every time I opened a letter, your neat writing and your sincere and artless words filled me with infinite joy and gratitude. Thanks to these letters, for the last few years I have never felt lonely — whether I was sick in bed, or living all alone, or on the journey — for I knew for sure that so many pure and innocent hearts are surrounding and following me on all sides!

Therefore, beginning on the first day of the 32rd year of the Republic of China, I will make use of some space in Ta Kung Pao to repay my young readers. This correspondence will be kept on. I hope that, with more experiences, what I'm going to contribute to you this time is broader in scope and deeper in significance.

I hope that this first letter brings a cheerful and joyous mood to every young reader!

I hope that the sixth New Year after the Anti-Japanese War is happier and brighter because of you!

Your friend,
Bing Xin

Letter 2

Chongqing
December 22nd, 1942

Little friends,

Today, let's talk about friendship.

Friendship is the most valuable human relationship. Although listed as the last item of the five human relationships, friends are the most comprehensive category of all, for the ruler (leader or boss, in today's terminology) and subject, father and son, brothers, and husband and wife can also be your friends.

Friends are not identified by nationality, age, or sex; as long as they have the same ideal and similar interests and are congenial and on harmonious terms, they can be linked by a

strong bond. The realization of noble ideals, the success of hard undertakings, and the creation of great art — countless instances of these are the joint effort of a group of friends with a common goal. It is by no means rare in all times and in all countries.

Not only do people with similar or the same personality tend to become friends, but friends also serve to give meaning to your moments of spiritual barrenness, to compensate for your regrets, and to deepen your soul. If you are a straightforward and uninhibited sort of person, you will admire more the modesty and depth of your friend; if you are an passionate and energetic sort of person, you will appreciate more the simplicity and calmness of your friend; if you are a sentimental and sickly sort of person, you will envy more the good shape and buoyancy of your friend. Different personalities are the different strings on a stringed instrument; when played harmoniously, it will produce heavenly resonance.

Making friends is an art.

An enthusiastic, lively, and sympathetic person tends to attract many friends. However, a magnet attracts only iron and steel, and the moon attracts only the tide.

If you know how to select friends, your friends will treasure your friendship much more than usual.

Don't always hope to get something from your friends; you should also think what your friends can get from you.

Only those who are willing to plough are likely to have a good harvest; only those who contribute are entitled to accept.

Friendship is a tranquillizer and a stimulant.

One who makes you degenerate or low-spirited is not your good friend. Meanwhile, be mindful of whether you are encouraging your friends and making them positive.

Friendship is a beacon on the sea and an oasis in the desert.

When the sailing boat of your heart has drifted to where "sense" and "desire" meet and is threatened by the surging waves and jagged rocks there, you want to seek the divine light, given out secretly by your friend, to illuminate and lead you. When you are on your life's journey, feeling hot, monotonous and tired out, your hard work unrecognized and unrewarded, you want to find shelter under the green shade of your friend and drink to your heart's content the sweet and refreshing spring water there.

As an ancient saying goes, "It is rarest that an old friend comes to visit us, braving wind and rain." Not only is there wind and rain in the physical world, but there is wind and rain in the spiritual world!

Has your soul ever lost its way in a deserted valley or in the wilderness, exposed to wind and rain and with no one in sight, when your friend opens the wicker gate of "sympathy," invites you to enter his thatched cottage of "love," takes off your rain cape of toil, wipes the tears from your cheeks, and has you seated by the warm fire of "friendship"?

Meanwhile, you should keep the gate of

sympathy open, make a fire of friendship, and look out in front of your house.

In friendship there is only happiness, consolation, encouragement, and connectedness.

Although there is also suffering in friendship — sentences lamenting the loss of friends are not lacking in ancient poetry and prose — friendship is immortal and it won't end because of parting or farewell. "So long as we remain bosom friends in our heart of hearts, / We'll still feel like neighbors despite the distance apart." "One will have no regrets about one's life if one has a bosom friend." The suffering in friendship does not include solitude, for we are enjoying the friendly sentiments of our friends. Solitude, the loneliness of one's heart, is the most terrible thing in the world!

Little friends, although we set out on our life's journey alone, we are joined, on the way, by many fellow travelers, who go forward hand in hand in an exultant mood, forming an orderly contingent which enables us to overcome the rugged and dangerously steep roads of the world and to forget the fatigue after a long journey. How shall we express our gratitude for such a relationship, for such a fate in the world?

I hope you are my good friends forever. If I am worthy of it, please allow me to be your good friend too.

Bing Xin

Letter 3

Geleshan
January 3rd, 1942

Dear little friends,

Last night the new moon was visible, but this morning it is heavily overcast again! All is quiet in the mountains. I have made a fire and closed the door of my study. On the desk by the window is a branch of wintersweet, a burning joss stick, and a cup of green tea. Supporting my head with a hand, I am sitting there trying hard to think about my mother.

Today is the eighth day of the twelfth lunar month, the day on which my mother used to think about her mother. Now it's my turn.

It has been thirteen years since my mother passed away. On this day in all those years, I would go out to divert myself rather than let loose my grief. Today, however, I decide to be sober and think deeply about my beloved mother.

Over the last thirteen years, my mother's voice and face have grown vaguer in my memory. It seems that I have been going down slowly from the highest peak, and every time I stop and look back, I find the mountain ever more towering and more solemn. I know, the further away I am from the mountain, the loftier it will become.

Deep pangs of sorrow abate over time. In the past 10-odd years, I have gained more experience of life, and even more of men. I feel keenly that the reason why I respect and love her is not that she is my mother, but that she has the noblest character among those I have met in all my life.

She was a sickly person, but physical illness

had never affected the soundness of her mind. She was a quiet person, but she used to be the initiator of all the laughter and lively activities around her. She had never been to any old-style private school or any public school, but she was able to appreciate traditional literature and accept new thoughts. She had no extra money all her life, but she was eager to help those in need. Before marriage, she was the only daughter in the family, who had been delicately brought up; but after marriage, in a large family of more than thirty people, she showed respect for the older and had tender affection for the younger, and everyone in the family respected and loved her. As far as decoration of the house was concerned, she preferred to make it neat and exquisite yet without a touch of luxury. As for the clothes she prepared for the

family, she favored simplicity and plainness but she avoided shabbiness. She had never been brusque with children or servants, but the whole family unanimously respected what she said. Her life, which had been spent with us, was worthy of what Father had said of her: "A cool breeze that blows among the seats, a moon that shines overhead." What rare self-cultivation! How magnanimous! What a great personality!

For the last thirteen years, Mother has always lived in our memory. At the family reunions or when some of us got together, there used to be a moment at which all of us became silent. Though we didn't say anything, we knew that, within that silent moment, we were each thinking about Mother with deep sorrow.

We thought of her while we were visiting places of scenic beauty; we thought of her while we were reading a good book; we thought of her when we heard a good discussion; we thought of her when we saw a beautiful person. If Mother had been alive and present on those occasions, I wonder what marvelous comments she would have made and what accurate judgments she would have given. We thought of her not only in time of happiness, but, even more so, in time of hardship. We were concerned about her health; while we were fleeing or running for shelter in air raids during the Anti-Japanese War, we all thought that, if Mother had been alive, her fragile health couldn't have withstood the terror and running about like that, and we all thanked God for letting her die earlier. But we also thought that, if Mother had been alive, we couldn't imagine how excited and enthusiastic she would have been and what great encouragement and comfort she would have given us — all this, however, is meaningless now.

In my life, Mother has been the person most capable of comforting and encouraging me with her spirit. Over the last 10-odd years, in my life as a teacher, a housewife, and a mother, I have also comforted and encouraged others with my spirit. When I was worn-out, agitated, or dispirited, my heart would become infinitely perplexed and hollow. I would think: if Mother were alive, even if I didn't utter a word, I would get infinite comfort and warmth, pluck up courage once more, and regain the energy to cope with everything, as long as I could rest on her shoulder and enjoy, with eyes closed, the tranquility brought by the gentle stroke she gave me. But the fact is: the void for the 10-odd years can never be filled — grief, the grief of losing Mother!

A wintersweet blossom falls silently onto the desk. The joss stick has burnt out, and the tea is cold! Also, the charcoal is reduced to ashes. Feeling a sudden shudder in my heart, I stand up, push open the window and look out. All is obscured. As it turns out, the fog has become denser! The fog condenses on pine branches. On the tips of millions of needles on thousands of pine trees stand millions of glistening teardrops...

Please forgive me for discontinuing writing. Little friends, if your mother is still alive, I hope that you always live in your mother's affection; if your mother has passed away, I hope that your mother's beauty and kindness always live in your personality!

Your friend,
Bing Xin

Letter 4

A rainy night on Geleshan
December 1st, 1944

Dear little friends,

A little friend who has joined the army asked me to talk about life. It is not easy to straighten out this issue.

I don't dare to say what life is; I can only say what life is like.

Life is like a river flowing eastward. It originated from the highest place, growing out of ice and snow. A myriad small streams are united to form a gigantic force and rush down, passing through cliffs and precipices, shattering layers of sandy soil, sweeping along tons of sand and stones. It runs along happily and bravely, enjoying everything it comes across on the way —

Sometimes, when it is confronted by an overhanging rock, it surges violently, roaring and circling, pressing forward with waves upon waves, until it rushes over and shatters the precipitous cliff, and then it races calmly down its long course.

Sometimes, when it is passing through

a beach of fine golden sand, on seeing, on the banks, bright red peach blossoms amidst fragrant grass illuminated by the setting sun, it is both happy and shy and flows on quietly, chanting in a low voice and light-heartedly bringing this romantic journey to an end.

Sometimes, it comes across a storm. The lightning flashes and sudden peals of thunder make it tremble with terror. Stirred up by fierce wind and assaulted by heavy rain, it temporarily becomes turbid and disturbed. But once the sun shines again after the storm, what it has experienced only lends more new force to it.

Sometimes, when the sunset clouds or the crescent moon shine or cast shadows upon it, with a trace of warmth in the chilly light, it only wants to take a rest or go to sleep, while the force pressing forward is still urging it to move on...

At last, there comes the day when it can see the ocean in the distance. Oh, it is nearing the end of its journey! The ocean forces it to hold its breath and lower its head. How vast and how great she is! How bright, yet how dark! The ocean solemnly holds out her arms to receive it, and it flows into her arms without a word. It melts; it is naturalized. There is neither happiness nor sadness in it!

Maybe one day it will rise again from the heavy rain on the sea, fly westward, again form a river, again shatter the cliffs, again come to look for the peach blossoms on the banks.

However, I don't dare to speak of the afterlife, and I don't believe in the afterlife!

Life is also like a small tree. It absorbs a lot of vitality from under the earth, stretch itself under ice and snow, and then, bravely and happily, break through the wet soil of early spring. It may be growing on the plain, in a rock, or on a city wall. Once it raises its eyes and sees the sky — Oh, sees the sky! — it will reach out its tender leaves to take in air, endure the sunshine, sing in the rain, and dance in the wind. Maybe it is being shaded by a big tree, or maybe it is being overshadowed by it, but the power of growth eventually enables it to get free from the branches and leaves over it and stand erect under the scorching sun!

Now it is spending the spring extravagantly. Perhaps it is in full blossom, and bees and butterflies are bustling around it and birds are singing on its branches. It will hear the lyrical voice of orioles, the weeping of cuckoos, and perhaps the screech of owls.

When in its prime, it shelters the flowers and grass underneath with its thick canopy. It bears countless fruit, which is a manifestation of the infinite sweetness and fragrance of the Earth.

Now, the autumn wind is blowing and turning its leaves from dark green to crimson. Under the autumn sun, it takes on solemnity and magnificence of a different kind: not the pride of blossoming or the happiness of bearing fruit, but the cheerful contentment of being successful!

Finally, the day comes when the north wind of the winter strips it of its yellow leaves and dry branches, and it shakes feebly in the air and moans under its roots. The Earth reaches out her hands to receive it, and it falls into her arms without a word. It melts; it is naturalized. There is neither happiness nor sadness in it!

Perhaps one day, it will break out of a nut in the soil and grow into a small tree again. Again, it will free itself of the shelter of big trees and listen to the singing of orioles.

However, I don't dare to speak of the afterlife, and I don't believe in the afterlife.

The universe is a great life, and we are a breath of the pervading air in the universe. A river flows into the ocean, and the falling leaves settle on the roots. We are a leaf and a drop of water in the great life.

How petty and insignificant we are in the great life of the universe! However, a single leaf or a single drop of water has its own mission!

Remember this: the symbol of life is activity and growth; the growth and activities of each leaf and each drop of water combine to form the evolution of the whole universe.

Bear this in mind: not every river runs into the ocean; those who refuse to flow become dead lakes. Not every seed grows into a tree; those who are unwilling to grow become hollow shells!

Life is not eternal happiness, nor is it eternal suffering. Happiness and suffering go hand in hand. Analogously speaking, a water course must pass through two different banks simultaneously, and trees must undergo the cycle of the seasons.

When happy, we should be grateful to life; when in suffering, we should also be grateful to life. Admittedly, happiness is exciting, but isn't suffering beautiful? I came across a memorable line somewhere, which goes: "May there be enough clouds in your life to make a beautiful sunset."

Today, there are more clouds than ever before in our personal lives, in our country, and in the world.

Little friends, do we long to have a happy memory after success, or, in the words of that poet, "a beautiful sunset"?

Best wishes from your friend,
Bing Xin

Beijing Opera and Children Who Perform Beijing Opera

I have loved Beijing opera since I was a child, although I can't appreciate it and rarely go to the theater. My story with Beijing opera began like this. When I was a small child, I lived in a quiet mountain village in Dongshan, Yantai, where the sky and the sea were joined together. As there were no companions to play with me, I spent most of the time reading books. I began to read *The Romance of the Three Kingdoms* at the age of seven. There were

not many children's books at that time, so I had to read a couple of well-known works repeatedly, such as *The Romance of the Three Kingdoms, A Journey to the West*, and *The Outlaws of the Marsh*. Therefore, I knew the plots and all the characters' names in those books thoroughly. Once, a friend of my father's invited us to go to the theater. To a child who had always stayed in a remote mountain area, going downtown was the biggest event! That occasion has left a very deep impression on me. I still remember that the theater was called "Immortals Tea Garden." They were staging the complete Three Kingdoms, which began with "The Gathering of Heroes" and "Borrowing Arrows" and ended with "The Huarong Valley," which were the most exciting part in *The Romance of the Three Kingdoms*. I was exhilarated to see my favorite characters, who looked dignified in their costumes, walk onto the stage one by one. I stood leaning over the railings for several hours. And I couldn't spare the time to answer my father when he patted me on the shoulder from behind and spoke to me.

From then on, I was in deep love with Beijing opera. I never let slip by the only one or two opportunities in a year to go to the theater, for only on the stage could I see my old friends Zhuge Liang, Sun Wukong, and Lin Chong.

At the age of twelve, I came to Beijing, the birthplace of Beijing opera. Our landlady, Madam Qi, was a theater fan, who would "listen to" the opera once or twice a week. She often invited my mother along; my mother was too weak to sit for a long time, so she would ask me to go instead of her. My first visit to the theater in Beijing has also left a very deep impression on me. That was the Auspicious Theater in Dong'an Market. At that time, female theater-goers sat upstairs, and male ones downstairs. Hot towels were thrown about in the stalls, and snacks like melon seeds and preserved fruit were served on tea tables. The last but one item on that day's performance was "Fenhe River Bend," performed by Mr. Mei Lanfang and Mr. Wang Fengqing. Even a child who didn't know how to appreciate Beijing opera as I was would go back home with the following appraisal: "Today's 'Fenhe River Bend' is terrific!"

After I went to school, I had at most one or two opportunities to go to the theater each year, but my passion for Beijing opera never waned. I read notes and books about Beijing opera that I could lay my hands on, and I read the "theatrical programs" and reviews on daily newspapers. From what I read, I had some understanding of the tradition of Beijing opera and what an operatic actor's life was like.

Twenty years ago, Mr. Jiao Juyin established a Beijing opera school in Beijing. Sometimes, I went to the Auspicious Theater to see the students' public performance. I enjoyed their performance very much! They were vigorous and energetic, and even those who played walk-on parts were conscientious. In addition, whatever character it was, one with a smaller size was especially amusing. The boorish "small" Zhangfei, with a very big face but very small hands and a small mouth uttering yells of "wayaya," was really charming.

Over the years, I have always wanted to visit a Beijing opera school and see the children's living and study conditions there. It was not until July 3rd this year that I had the opportunity to visit the Traditional Opera School of Beijing. I was so happy to have my long-cherished wish fulfilled.

Our car stopped in front of a tall building in the Traditional Opera School of Beijing. While we were waiting for the person in charge, I looked up at the wall newspaper on the corridor wall and at the children with red scarves coming in and out, and I were hardly aware that I was in a traditional opera school. Mr. Hong, Dean of Studies, came out and said Headmaster Hao was administering an exam for first-year students. He asked us if we would like to go over there and have a look. Of course we'd love to. We went out of this building and walked towards another large building. We could hear the sounds of huqin and percussion instruments from a distance. The atmosphere of traditional opera was becoming more apparent.

This was the rehearsal hall of the school. First-year students were having a dress rehearsal on the stage. Teachers who gave them appraisals were sitting in two rows in front of the stage. We were greeted by a hale and hearty old man with a ruddy complexion. He turned out to be none other than Mr. Hao Shouchen. Over twenty years ago, I attended a performance of "Lianhuantao," featuring Mr. Hao and Mr. Yang Xiaolou. So, I have heard about Mr. Hao for a long, long time!

As soon as I sat down quietly on the chair next to him, Mr. Hao turned his head toward the stage again and concentrated on the performance. On the stage there were four students of about eleven or twelve years old. They were performing "Saving the Country," in which the officals Xu Yanzhao and Yang Bo struggled against Li Liang, father of the empress regent, in the presence of the imperial concubine. Mr. Hao's lips were moving throughout the performance, as if he was silently leading them in singing each character and each line. He was tapping his knee to the rhythm of the music with a folding fan. His concentration, conscientiousness, and cordiality touched us and inspired our respect.

After sitting in on a performance of "Saving the Country," we went out to visit the school buildings.

The former school buildings were a mere compound in the style of a temple. Outside the school gate was a public cemetery for operatic actors. It is said that Mr. Yang Xiaolou, Mr. Jin Xiushan, and some other famous actors were buried there. But now the cemetery has moved to somewhere else. This school was formerly known as

Yipei School, which was established by the Beijing Opera Guild in 1952. Mr. Mei Lanfang, president of the board of directors, Mr. Hao Shouchen, and Mr. Xiao Changhua gave benefit performances and raised a fund of over five thousand yuan. Dozens of students were enrolled, of whom forty percent were children of operatic actors. At that time, there were only professional teachers; there were no teachers for general knowledge courses. For lack of funds, some students started to give commercial performances after only four months' training in order to cover the expense. The Party has always attached great importance to educating actors of Beijing opera, which is loved greatly by the people. After the government took over the school, the buildings have multiplied, teachers have increased, etc. Now, students are engaged in vocational study in the morning and take general knowledge courses in the afternoon – not so different from a regular school. There are three classes in the first, fourth, and seventh grades respectively; altogether, there are over a hundred seventy students. Among the students of the proper age, eighty percent are Young Pioneers. This year, there are altogether sixty-two actors in the graduate classes and the rest are music students. They will be assigned, respectively, to the opera troupes of Mei Lanfang, Xun Huisheng, and Shang Xiaoyun. It is said that Mr. Mei has already been here to choose disciples.

We stepped into another building which resembled a gymnasium. Some students were turning somersaults and throwing weapons back and forth on a very thick mat. Wearing broad smiles on their ruddy cheeks, they were merely teenagers between eleven and fourteen years old.

Finally, we had a talk with several eighth-year students in an office. These young people, both male and female, are less than twenty years old, the youngest being seventeen. We had a cordial and animated talk. Some of them are operatic actors' children, who have a natural love for Beijing opera; others showed an interest in it at a very early age. As Ba Jinling, a *huadan* student, said, "I loved singing and dancing, and especially Beijing opera, when I was in primary school. When the school began to enroll new students, I signed up. My mother had refused to let me come, because she was afraid we would take beatings. After a three-month probation period, it was clear that there was no corporal punishment here, so my parents finally agreed." They also mentioned the difficulties and problems in their study, but they managed to overcome them with the guidance of teachers and through their own efforts. For instance, the *laodan* student Wang Xiaolin at first didn't like the role of an old woman. She said smilingly, "When I knew I was assigned to study *laodan*, I really hated it. At that time I only liked the role of a young woman who can use makeup and wear flowers. Then my teacher told me my voice was suitable for *laodan*. I trusted our experienced teacher, so I devoted myself to my study and now – I'm really in love with this role!"

Their efforts are not in vain. In the evening the next day, I attended their performance. Some of the students we had talked with were on the stage that evening, such as Lin Maorong, who played the part of Zhou Yu in "Reed Marshes," Li Yufu, who played the part of Lian Jinfeng in "Stabbing the Clam," and Zhang Xuejin, who played the part of Liu Bei in "Tower of Yellow Crane." Recalling how they looked off stage, I appreciated greatly their performance on the stage. Wang Xiaolin, who played the part of Kou Zhun's wet nurse, displayed the character and status of her role with great delicacy and sensibility. She had facial expressions befitting her role and, what's more, she had a good voice.

The whole performance was quite successful. Not only were there no empty seats, but there were a lot of people outside the gates. The audience liked these little actors; a beautiful piece of vocal music or a few somersaults done successively would win appreciation and applause of encouragement...

Beijing opera is one of the favorite national forms of art of the people, and Beijing operatic actors are forever admired and paid attention to by the masses. But who does not know the hardships of actors before Liberation? It is not groundless that Ba Jinling's mother had misgivings. In the past, children would receive countless tongue-lashings and beatings and endure infinite torment if they were going to learn traditional opera. Even when they became famous, the vicious old society would use every means to force them to embark on the road of humiliation and degeneration...

The little actors in the era of Mao Zedong are happy. They are like flowers thriving in the bright sunshine. I hope that they live up to the expectations of the Party and the people, who love and care for them; that they treasure the happy and peaceful environment and, under the instructions of great teachers, study diligently and practice hard; and that they, when they have mastered the skills, perform on the stage the historical stories of life and struggle and the familiar characters that the people love to see in a more vivid and powerful way.

The Spring Festivals in My Childhood

In my childhood, there were not only solitary wanderings at the seaside and in the mountains, but also occasions of hustle and bustle, that is, the "lunar New Year" as it was called in the past or the "Spring Festival" as it is now called.

At that time, our home was located in the southeastern part of the mountain behind Yantai Naval Academy. We lived in a most out-of-the-way area: there were only a few villages nearby. To go to Yantai City, we had to climb over the Eastern Mountain. Nevertheless, the New Year was the most important holiday in a year.

In the few days before the New Year, Mother was the busiest person in our family. She was busy preparing the new clothes, shoes and hats that we were going to wear on the New Year's day; she was busy preparing meat enough for the whole family to eat in the next fifteen days, because according to the custom there, from the lunar New Year's Day through the 15th day of that month, they did not kill pigs and sell meat. I saw Mother tie an apron, roll up her sleeves, fill a big jar with big cubes of delicious pickled meat wrapped in red wine dregs, stew seasoned meat in soy sauce with sugar and all kinds of herbs and spices, steam brown-sugar New Year cake in several food steamers... As Mother was doing all this, not only were we children standing beside her with greedy eyes, but the cook and Auntie Yu, who were helping out.

As for Father, he was in charge of preparing New Year entertainments for the children who came back from school. Both my cousin on the paternal side and my cousin on the maternal side went to the naval academy. "A cousin is three thousand miles away." Quite true. The son of your father's sister, the son

of your mother's brother, the son of your mother's sister – there were seven or eight of them. Father bought a set of instruments from Yantai City: gong and drum, bamboo flute and vertical bamboo flute, erhu and yueqin... When played together, they made wonderfully loud music. The pity was I was not allowed in their band! I could do nothing but play firecrackers in the day and play fireworks at night – both were bought by Father. The big fireworks were to be placed on the ground to be set off. How dazzling were the displays of fiery trees and silver flowers! But what I loved most was a kind of tiny and plain fireworks called "golden drops." It was a spill of rolled paper with a bit of gunpowder in it; it could be held in hand and, when lit, it would make some noise and send out sparks.

I remember that we put on new clothes and new shoes and worshipped ancestors first thing on the lunar New Year's Day. (Our family didn't worship Buddha or immortals – on the altar table there were only memorial tablets of ancestors, joss sticks, candles, and sacrificial offerings, which would be our lunch on New Year' Day.) Then, we wished our parents and elders a Happy New Year. The money

I received in red envelopes was mostly 1-dollar Mexican silver dollars which bore a "standing man" on one side, and I asked Mother to take care of the money for me.

The most engaging activity was the entertainment gathering called "Flower Fair." The actors were farmers from nearby villages who were in the slack winter season. The programs included "boat that runs on land," "Aunt Wang mending a big jar," and that sort of thing. Those who played female characters were all young villagers who wore heavy make-up. On hearing the strains of music accompanied by drumbeats, a crowd of children clustered behind them. When they were passing our doorstep, a large crowd of people gathered around and an audience was formed naturally. Thus, they started their performance, singing and dancing to the accompaniment of instruments. The songs, which were usually funny and hilarious, sent us laughing a lot. When they had finished, we expressed our thanks by bringing them cigarettes, alcohol, and refreshments. As the flower fair of one village was just leaving, that of another village arrived – the earliest to come was, of course, that of

Jingouzhai Village, which was the nearest to us.

When I was eleven, I came back to my hometown, Fuzhou, Fujian Province. The lunar New Year there was much more exciting. There were altogether four branches in our extended family. Living under the same roof, we had meals separately, but Grandfather ate with our branch. From the 23rd day of the 12th lunar month on, we got busy tidying the house, cleaning doors and windows and copper and tin utensils, and preparing pickled chicken, ducks, fish, and meat. Grandfather was engaged in writing New Year couplets and putting them up on the well-wiped gate or side doors. On the morning of the New Year's Day, he wrote on a piece of red paper: "Beginning writing first thing in a year brings good luck..." The rest of the auspicious words I couldn't recognize, nor can I remember.

In the New Year, we received a lot of good stuff from the family of our respective maternal grandmother. To begin with, there was "kitchen stove sugar" and "kitchen stove cake," i.e., candies and pastries in boxes, which were used as sacrificial offerings to the kitchen god. Both the candies and pastries were very sweet and sticky; the purpose was to stick the kitchen god's mouth shut so that he could not speak ill of the household when he returned to Heaven. The best thing, however, was the lantern (denglong). In the Fuzhou dialect, deng (lantern) and ding (members of a family) are homophones; therefore, when people gave lanterns to children as presents, there was invariably one more lantern than the children there were, which symbolizes having a boy born into the family. At that time, my younger brothers were too small to scramble with me for the additional lantern. These lanterns were made of paper, gauze, glass, etc. So, on the wall of my room hung a running horse lantern, on which was painted "The Three Brothers Fighting against Lu Bu"; I carried in one hand a gold-fish lantern with movable eyes; and I drew with the other hand a white-rabbit lantern with wheels under the rabbit's feet. Besides, the Southern Back Street, on which our house was located, was a lantern fair; most of the stores on this street sold lanterns. Just outside the gate of our house was Wanxing's Barrels & Jewels, which sold all kinds of lanterns in addition to barrels of different sizes, all painted red and framed with gold wire, used as dowry. The lanterns they sold were not toys for children to play with, but large glass lanterns, gauze lanterns, mineral silk lanterns, horn lanterns, etc., on which were flower-and-bird and figure paintings with fine workmanship. On the New Year's Eve, all the lanterns were lit – As the line in Ouyang Xiu's poem said, "The lanterns at the bazaar were as bright as daylight" – and the street was thronged with people and their cheerful laughter.

After the 15th of the first lunar month, the most brilliant days in a year were over. The adults asked us to put the lanterns we had grown tired of into a pile to be burned. They said, "From tomorrow on, get your mind off play and concentrate on study." We listened in silence and gazed, with reluctance, at the embers of the lanterns in the courtyard, mixed with an unspeakable despondency and loneliness. Then, we went to bed. That night was really awful!

January 31, 1985

Separation

The hand of a Great Spirit delivered me from an oppressive, painful, and airtight net. I let out the first cry of misery.

Opening my eyes, I saw myself upside down, one of my legs still held in the hand of that Great Spirit and my two translucently red hands waving in the air above my head.

The hand of another Great Spirit was gently holding my waist. Smilingly, he turned his head toward the woman lying on her back on a white wheeled litter and said, "Congratulations! What a chubby boy!" Meanwhile, he placed me gently in a small basket padded with a piece of white cloth.

I struggled to look out. I saw a scene of confusion, in which a lot of nurses in white clothes and white caps were surrounding that woman silently. Her pale face was soaked in sweat. She was moaning softly, as if she had just woken up from a nightmare. Her eyelids were red and swollen,

and her blank eyes half open. At the words of the doctor, her eyes rolled and tears brimmed over. Feeling immensely relieved, she closed her eyes with a weary smile. "You must be very tired," she said to them.

Upon this, I cried loudly, "Mother! It is we who are tired – we have barely managed to come back from death!"

In a hurried and confused manner, the nurses in white pushed the wheeled litter out of the room in silence. I was lifted up and taken out of the room. With a doctor's beckoning, from the other end of the corridor came a man. He was joyous, as if he had also just woken up from a nightmare. He reached out his hands as if to hold me but dare not to, and he looked at me with wonder and tenderness. The doctor smiled. "What a lovely boy!" he said. The man felt a little embarrassed and said hesitantly, "His head is exceedingly long." Suddenly I felt great pain in my head and started crying again, "Father! You don't know how painful it was to squeeze my head out."

"Good gracious!" the doctor said with a smile. "What a big voice!" The nurse standing beside him smiled and took me from him.

We went into a big room bathed in sunshine. Around the room, placed side by side, were a lot of white cots, in which many little friends were lying. Some of them raised their hands to both sides of their head and were fast asleep; some were crying, "I'm thirsty!" "I'm hungry!" "I'm too hot!" "I'm wet!" The nurse who was holding me walked past their cots calmly and light-footedly, as if she hadn't heard what they were saying. She went into the bathroom and laid me down on the marble table next to the wash-basin, with my head toward the hose.

Warm water from the shower nozzle was sprinkled over my head, washing off all the slimy blood. A shiver ran over my body, and at once I became fully conscious. I looked up and saw on the other marble table across from the wash-basin was lying another little friend, who was being washed by another nurse. He had a round head, big eyes, dark skin, and a strong chest. He was also awake and was looking at the sky out of the window quietly. Now I was lifted up, and the nurse supported my back gently and dressed me in long white clothes. The little friend was also dressed. We stared at each other across the wash-basin. The nurse who had washed me spoke to her colleague with a smile, "Your boy is so big and so strong, but not as fair and beautiful as mine!" At that moment, the little friend raised his head and stared at me, wearing a smile of mixed pity and belittlement on his face.

I was ashamed and said in a soft voice, "Hello, little friend." "Hello, little friend," he replied modestly. Now we had been placed in two cots next to each other, and the nurses were gone.

"I'm aching all over," I said. "The struggle in the last four hours wasn't easy. How about you?"

He smiled and clenched his little hands. "Not for me," he answered. "I had been stifled for only half an hour. I didn't suffer. My mother didn't suffer, either."

Speechless, I let out a weary sigh and looked around. He comforted me. "You are tired," he said. "Get some sleep. I need some rest too."

Someone took me in her arms and carried me as far as the big glazed door. In the corridor outside the gate stood several young men and women, who were pressing their palms and noses against the glass, as if they had been children standing outside a showcase with Christmas gifts in it, greedy and envious. They were pointing at each other merrily and passing comments, saying that my eyebrows looked like those of my father's sister's, my eyes those of my mother's brother's, nose that of my father's brother's, mouth that of my mother's sister's — as if they were planning to dismember me and then gobble me up.

I closed my eyes and tried hard to shake my head, only to find my neck in pain. I cried bitterly, saying, "I'm only myself. I don't look like anybody! Take me away and let me have a rest!"

The nurse smiled and turned back. I could see them looking back from time to time as they went out, smiling and jostling each other.

The little friend had woken up. He greeted me. "You're up again. Who's come to see you?" he asked. As I was being put down, I said, "I don't know. Aunts and uncles, perhaps. All very young. They seem to love me very much."

The little friend kept silent for a while and then smiled again. "How lucky you are," he said. "We've been here for two days, but I haven't met my father yet."

I didn't realize that I had slept for such a long time. Now I felt the pain somewhat alleviated, but I was wet underneath. I learned to cry sobbingly, "I'm wet! I'm wet!" Indeed, a nurse came before long and took me in her arms. I was just about to rejoice when she fed me with water.

It was about dusk when I heard a commotion, and three or four nurses came in, their stiff white uniforms rustling softly. They held us in their arms and changed our diapers one by one. The

little friend was glad. "We are all going to see our mothers," he said. "See you."

He was pushed out with the rest of them on a large wheeled litter. I was carried out in a nurse's arms. Walking through the glazed door, we arrived at the first room on the right side of the corridor. Mother was lying on a very tall white bed, and she greeted me with expectant and joyous eyes. The nurse placed me in her arms, and she unbuttoned her shirt hesitantly. She looked quite young. Her jet-black hair was tied back, and her eyebrows were thin and curved, like a crescent moon. Her big, black eyes were set off by a pale, colorless face, which resembled a marble statue under the dim light of the bedside lamp.

I opened my mouth and sucked at my mother's breast. She leaned her cheek against my hair, fondled my fingers, and looked at me attentively — as if she was filled with pleasure and wonder.

Twenty minutes had passed, but I had got nothing from sucking. Feeling hungry and painful on the tip of the tongue, I opened my mouth, released the nipple, and cried out in vexation. Mother was terrified; she kept on patting and swinging me. "Don't cry, my dear," she said. "Don't cry!" Meanwhile, she rang the bell and a nurse came in. Mother said with a smile, "It's just that I've got no milk and the baby keeps on crying. What shall I do?" The nurse smiled. "Don't worry," she said. "You'll have milk sooner or later. The baby is too small to care for it." With these words, she reached out her arms, and Mother released me reluctantly.

When I came back to my bed, the little friend was already in bed. He was sound asleep and smiled from time to time in his dreams. It seemed that he was very contented and very happy. I looked around. Many little friends were sleeping happily. There were a few who were half awake; they cried a little, as if for fun. I was starved and I did care when my mother would have milk, but no one knew what was on my mind. Seeing everyone well-fed and sound asleep, I was at once jealous and ashamed, and I cried loudly in the hope of catching people's attention. I cried for about half an hour before a nurse came up. She pouted her lips in a lovely and innocent manner and patted me comfortingly. "Indeed!" she said. "Since your mom can't feed you to your heart's content, drink some water then!"

She inserted the nipple of a bottle into my mouth. With the nipple in my mouth, I whimpered softly until I finally fell asleep.

The next day, while we were taking a shower, the little friend and I lay on each side of the wash-basin and had a chat. He was full of vitality. As his head was pressed down to be washed, he shook his head, with his eyes half closed, and said smilingly, "Yesterday, I drank milk to my heart's content! My mother has a round, dark face. It's very beautiful. I'm her fifth child. She told the nurse that it was the first time that she had given birth to a child in the hospital, and that she came here on the recommendation of the Salesian Society. My father's very poor. He's a butcher, who kills pigs." In that very instant, a drop of boric acid solution spilled into one of his eyes. He uttered a few cries of detestation and struggled to open his eyes again. "Who kills pigs," he continued. "How gratifying it is to thrust in a glinting blade and pull it out dripping with blood! When I grow up, I'll follow my father's trade and kill pigs – not only pigs, but those who do nothing but eat, just like pigs!"

I had been listening silently. At that point, I

closed my eyes hastily and said nothing.

"How about you?" the little friend asked. "Have you had enough? How's your mother?"

I became interested. "I ate little," I said. "For my mother hasn't got milk yet. The nurse says she will in one or two days." "My mother is great," I continued. "She reads; there are a lot of books on her bedside table. And there are flowers all around the room."

"And your father?"

"Father was not there. She was alone in the room. Neither did she talk to anyone, so I know nothing about my father."

"That's a VIP ward," the little friend said decisively. "One room for one patient only! My mother's ward is noisy – there're a dozen or so beds. Many little friends' mothers are there, and they all have enough to suckle."

The next day, I saw my father. While I was suckling, he was leaning on Mother's pillow. They looked at me attentively, their faces very close to each other. My father had a thin face, yellowish-complexioned, with long eyelashes and very keen eyesight. As if he was given to deep thought, there often appeared fine wrinkles on his forehead.

Father said, "This time I have observed closely. What a beautiful child! He takes after you!"

Mother smiled and stroked my cheeks tenderly. "He also takes after you," she said. "Look at those big eyes."

Father stood up and sat down on the chair beside the bed. He held my mother's hand in his and patted it gently. "Now we won't feel lonely any more," he said. "When the class is over, I'll come to help you take care of him and play with him; during the vacations, I'll take him to go sightseeing. We must look after his health so that he doesn't become like me. Though I'm in good health, I'm not strong enough..."

My mother nodded. "Yes. He'd better start learning music and painting at an early age. As I myself can't do these things, I feel my life is imperfect! And..."

Father smiled. "What kind of specialist do you wish him to be in the future? A writer? A musician?"

"Whatever he becomes it'll be fine," Mother said. "He's a boy. China needs scientists. I'm afraid being a scientist is the best choice."

Meanwhile, I was so annoyed that I felt like crying, because I couldn't suck any milk out. However, as they were talking with such great interest, I had to keep silent.

Father said, "We should save money for his education from now on – the earlier the better."

And Mother said, "I forgot to tell you that my younger brother said yesterday that he'll give our child a small bicycle when he's six!"

Father smiled. "This child has got virtually everything he needs," he said. "Isn't his cradle given by my younger sister?"

Mother held me tightly in her arms and kissed my hair. "My little darling," she said. "How lucky you are, being loved by so many people! When you grow up, you must behave yourself and be a good boy..."

Beaming with joy, I went back to my bed in complete disregard of my empty stomach. I looked up at the little friend, and he was pondering again.

I greeted him with a smile. "Little friend, I saw my father," I said. "He's also very nice. He's a teacher. He and Mother were discussing my education in the future. Father said he'll try every means to procure everything that's good for me. Mother said it doesn't matter if she's got no milk. I can eat milk powder as soon as I get home, and when I'm a little older I have orange juice to drink and..." I went on without a break.

The little friend smiled, and his expression was one of mixed pity and contempt. "What a happy life you are having!" he said. "After I'm home, I won't have any milk. My father came today, and he told Mother that someone has hired her as a wet nurse. We are leaving in one or two days! I'll live with my grandmother, who's in her sixties. I'll eat rice water, rice flour... Well, I don't care!"

I fell silent, my feeling of cheerfulness vanished completely, and then I felt ashamed.

There was pride and courage in his eyes. "You will always be a little flower in the greenhouse," he said. "Blooming delicately in an environment of uniform temperature and proof against wind and rain. I am a blade of grass by the roadside. I have to endure people's trampling as well as violent storms. Perhaps you will pity me when you look out of the windows. Above my head, however, there is an infinite sky; around me, there is inexhaustible air. Free butterflies fly around me and unrestrained crickets sing beside me. My humble and brave companions cannot be burnt out or cut off altogether. Under people's feet, we have decorated the whole world with greenness!"

I was almost crying with embarrassment. "I don't want to be so delicate!..." I said.

The little friend gave a start, as if waking up from a dream. He eased up and comforted me. "Sure. No one wants to be different from others, but all kinds of things separate us — just wait and see!"

Outside the windows, snow was falling like masses of cotton; it piled up on the green-glazed tiles, forming several well-spaced snow grooves. Mother and I would be home for the New Year holiday. As his mother had to go to work, the little friend would leave before the New Year holiday, too. We had only a half day left. We were about to vanish, separately, into the vast anonymous mass of the population of a clamorous, chaotic city. When could we meet again and sleep side by side under the same roof?

We looked at each other fondly. In the twilight,

my eyes grew dim and his face seemed to be magnified. His lips tightened, his brows snapped together, his eyes gazed into space, and his chin was tilted slightly, all of which manifested his bravery and determination. "He kills pigs, or rather, humans?" At that thought, my little hands stretched and withdrew involuntarily under my quilt. Now I saw how small I was!

Having come back from our mothers' respective wards, we informed each other of the latest news and found that both of us were going home tomorrow – the first day of the first lunar month! My father was afraid that my mother couldn't get any rest if they came back on New Year's Eve, as it would be a very busy day. The little friend's father would go out to avoid creditors on New Year's Eve, so he told his wife to stay in the hospital so that she would not be surrounded by creditors if she came home today. That meant we had one more day left!

From midnight on, incessant explosions of firecrackers could be heard far and near. Through the drifting snow came a few barks of dogs, which seemed to tell us that another debt of gratitude and of revenge was settled now. Before masks of modesty and happiness were put on once more the next day, tonight let them gobble, rail, and weep to their hearts' content. Amid the explosions of millions of firecrackers and in the gloomy streets and lanes lurked innumerable horrifying, turbulent feelings...

I shuddered. I turned round and found the little friend biting his lower lip and speechless. The night went by slowly, like a sluggish flow of the water. It was approaching dawn. In the dim light, I heard the little friend sighing in his bed.

The day grew strong. Two nurses came in, beaming with New Year greetings, and gave us our bath. One of them opened my little suitcase, and put on for me a small white flannel close-fitting undergarment and then a long white flannel waistcoat and pajama, over which was a pea green woolen short gown. My hat and socks were also pea green. Having dressed me, she took me in her arms and said smilingly, "What a beautiful boy! Look how stylish these clothes are that your mother has prepared for you!" The clothes were soft and comfortable, yet I felt very hot in them, and I grew

so agitated that I felt like crying.

The little friend was also lifted up. I was dumbfounded, for I could hardly recognize him! He was wearing a large, thick blue denim cotton-padded jacket with exceedingly long, loose sleeves, on which stitches of patchwork were visible, and washed-out dungarees. Arms fully stretched out and head buried in a large dark green cotton hat, he looked as bulky as a kite! Looking down at the same white clothes that we two had taken off lying on the floor, I couldn't help shivering. Now we were separated, both physically and mentally, separated once and for all!

The little friend saw me and flashed a smile of mixed pride and shame. "You look great in those warm and beautiful clothes! What I wear is my suit of armor, for I have to compete with others to earn a livelihood on the battlefield of society."

Hurriedly, the nurses picked up the white clothes on the floor and threw them into a basket. Hurriedly, they held us in their arms and went out. When we arrived at the glazed door, I couldn't help crying; neither could the little friend. We waved our hands wildly and said to each other, "Little friend, goodbye! Goodbye!" We went our separate ways, and the sounds of our crying disappeared at the two ends of the corridor.

Mother was already dressed and was standing at the door of her ward. Father was beside her, a small suitcase in hand. At the sight of me, Mother reached out her arms hastily and received me. She looked at my face closely, wiped my tears, and snuggled up to me. "Don't cry, my boy!" she said. "We're going home, a happy home. Both Mom and Dad love you!"

A wheelchair was pushed in. Mother wrapped a pea-green flannel blanket around me before sitting into the wheelchair, with me in her arms. Father followed us. Having expressed our thanks and said goodbye to the doctors and nurses, we went down by elevator.

Through the glazed double doors I saw a car parked outside. Father caught up and opened the door. Flakes of snow were blown in, and Mother covered my face immediately. After, it seemed that we got up from the wheelchair, walked out of the doors, and went into the car, and that the car door slammed. Mother took off the blanket from my face, and I found the car was filled with flowers. I was in

Mother's arms, and their faces were nestling against mine.

Now, the car was driving slowly out of the gate, which was blocked up by many cars out there. The cars were trying to make way when I raised my head and suddenly saw the little friend with whom I had stayed from morning to night for ten days! He was in his father's arms. His mother was carrying a black cloth-wrapper. They were standing sideways beside the gate, with their backs toward us. His father wore a black broad-brim felt hat and a large black cotton-padded robe. The little friend leaned on his father's shoulder, his face toward me, and snow was falling on his brows and cheeks. He kept his eyes tight shut, and on his face was a smile of sadness and pride... He had already begun to enjoy his struggles!...

Once outside the gate, our car sped along the road. Flakes of snow were dancing in the air. There was a faint sound of gongs and drums of the New Year. "My dear," Mother whispered in my ear. "Look at this smooth, pure white world!"

I wept.

Haidian; August 5th, 1931

Good Mother

This morning, my youngest brother and sister woke me up. The former said the latter had taken his socks, and the latter blamed the former for wearing her clothes. They stood on the bed pushing and pulling, and many clothes were tossed onto the floor. "Mother," I shouted hastily. "Come quickly! They are quarrelling again. They simply won't let me get some more sleep even on Sunday morning!"

Father came in from the outer room and said in a low voice, "Don't make so much noise. Your mom is cooking breakfast. Leave her in peace for a while, will you?" So saying, he helped to dress them and took them out.

I got into bed again and closed my eyes tightly, but I simply couldn't fall asleep. Remembering that I had to take part in the Young Pioneers' activities this afternoon, I wondered if Mother had washed my uniform or not. There was too much homework to do in the morning. Sunday is always the busiest day for me in a week!

Thinking of all this, I could no longer remain in bed, so I got up quickly, put on my clothes, pushed the quilt aside, and went to wash my face and comb my hair in a hurry. I grabbed the food from the table and ate hastily. "Have you washed the uniform I took off yesterday?" I asked Mother. "I need to wear it for the Young Pioneers' activities this afternoon."

Mother was tidying up the room and my words baffled her. "Haven't you worn it for just a couple of days?" she asked. "How come it's dirty again?"

I grew anxious. "That's true," I said. "But one of the sleeves was blotted with ink by one of my classmates. I took it off last night but I forgot to tell

you. Anyway, I can't wear it like that to school. It's so ugly!"

"All right," Mother sighed. "I'll wash it as soon as I've finished my work. But it may not dry in time. How come you take part in the Young Pioneers' activities again? I'm occupied this afternoon and I'm counting on you to look after your little brother and sister for me."

I opened my eyes wide and shook my head. "No way!" I said. "We mustn't be absent from the Young Pioneers' activities! You're always occupied on Sunday, but I have my business too. You simply don't have any plans. Our teacher tells us that we should learn how to arrange our time. If we do everything in a planned way, we won't be in a hurry. I advise you to make plans in the future!"

Father came up and said, "How could your mother make plans if you didn't tell her earlier that you got your clothes dirty after wearing it for only a couple of days and that you would take part in the Young Pioneers' activities today?"

I put down the bowl and went into the inner room without saying anything. I had to make haste and do some homework; I wouldn't have any time in the afternoon.

When I came in, my youngest brother and sister were rummaging my schoolbag. They had taken out everything in it – the books, the pencil-box, etc. I hastened to push them away. While I was putting my books in order, I found the arithmetic book missing. Feeling annoyed, I cried out again, "Mother, come here and look! How nasty they are! They are touching my things again! And my arithmetic book is missing!" Mother stepped in, "It is you who placed that book on the table," she said. "And I have put it into the drawer. You never put your own books in order or hang your schoolbag up, and you blame your little brother and sister for touching your things!"

Meanwhile, the two little things had slipped out of the room, and Father had taken them out to play.

I took the arithmetic book out of the drawer in a huff and was going to sit down and do a few exercises, only to find the table laden with things – cups, books, a thermos bottle and what not. There was no room left at all!

Chaos, utter chaos! Mother is always having many things to attend to at the same time. God knows what she's busy with. The house is always in a mess! That's why I admire our neighbor Aunt Li. Their house is always neat and tidy, and so are the clothes Li Yongzhen wears. They have more children than we have, but I have never seen Aunt Li in a muddle.

I thought: Why not go to their place and do my homework there? It's always quiet there and their children are not noisy. Uncle Li likes us, and he often talks and laughs with us. Besides, Yongzhen will help me with my homework. With these thoughts, I grabbed my books and ran toward the Lis.

As I stepped into their house, I found it had already been tidied up. Yongying, Yongzhen's elder sister, is a high school student. She was home today and was wiping a table. Yongzhen was drawing pictures on the desk with her youngest brother and sister. Uncle Li and Aunt Li were changing clothes in the inner room; they seemed to be going out. When Aunt Li saw me, she greeted me smilingly. "Good morning, Xiaoqin!" she said. "You are a good student; you work hard even on Sunday. What's your mother doing?" "She's tidying up the house," I said. "You are going out so early?" "Yes," Aunt Li responded. "Yongzhen said today's morning show at the cinema was very good, so your uncle went to buy the tickets in the early morning and said he would go with me. I said there were many people home and many things to do on Sunday and I'd better stay home, but they insisted." Uncle

Li smiled. "When there're many people," he said. "There should be fewer things to do. Sunday is supposed to be the day for rest. We workers don't go to work on Sunday; students don't go to school on Sunday. Only you housewives are busy throughout the year without any rest." Turning round, he said to Yongying with a smile, "You often write home, saying, 'Dear Mother, are the new shoes ready? I'll take them with me on Sunday, for my shoes are broken again.' Or, 'Dear Mother, I want to eat dumplings. Can you prepare some for me this Sunday?' You take it for granted that on Sunday, when all of us have a day off, your dear mother is supposed to work overtime, do you?"

Yongying smiled. "No," she said. "It's been more than a year since I asked Mother to make shoes for me. Now I can do it myself!"

Yongzhen also smiled. "No," she said. "Now we all help Mother out every day!"

Their youngest brother and sister shouted merrily, "No, no! We all behave ourselves now. We're not noisy and we no longer pester Mother to bring us along when she goes out."

Uncle Li said, "That's right. You should not only be

a good student and a good Young Pioneer at school, but be a good child at home. Only in this way..."

"They are great helpers now," Aunt Li interrupted him. "You needn't say too much."

Both Yongying and Yongzhen smiled. "OK, dear Mother," they said. "You'd better go now; otherwise, you might miss the movie."

Aunt Li stood up. "Then we're leaving," she said. "Let's have sautéed noodles with minced meat for lunch today. Both the meat and the bean sauce are in the cupboard."

Yongying smiled. "We know," she said. "We won't forget it. You'll find the

noodle ready when you come back at noon."

Uncle Li went out at the heels of Aunt Li with a broad smile on his face. Their little children chased out of the door and shouted merrily, "Goodbye, Mom!"

As soon as their parents went out, Yongying asked Yongzhen, "Where has Mom hidden the pile of dirty clothes we took off last night? As there's nothing else to do in the morning, let me wash them."

"Let Mom wash them," Yongzhen replied. "Every week you come home, you stay for only a day or even half a day. You should have a good rest or do some homework. She said she'll wash those clothes tomorrow when she's not busy. She asked me not to let you wash them."

Yongying said, "I've finished all my homework. To help Mom with housework is part of my schedule; it won't interfere with my work at all. I'll chat with you while I wash the clothes; that's as good as rest."

Yongzhen went into the room and returned with a pile of clothes in her arms. And Yongying sat in a corner of the room and started washing them.

Yongzhen helped me to sit down at the desk and asked me which subject I was going to review. I said I was going to do the arithmetic exercises and asked her if she would like to join me in doing these exercises. "I've finished the arithmetic exercises," Yongzhen said. "But I can help you." With these words, she fetched the iron that was being heated on the stove and started to iron the uniform she was going to wear for the Young Pioneers' activities this afternoon; meanwhile, she answered my questions.

I was doing the arithmetic exercises with my head lowered, but I was feeling ghastly. It was extremely quiet in the room, and I could only hear the rustling sound of Yongying washing clothes and Yongzhen ironing clothes. I thought, "I used to compare Mom with Aunt Li and thought Aunt Li was much more competent than Mom, but until today I didn't know Yongzhen and Yongying had done so much for their mother! Now Yongzhen's mother has gone to the cinema, while my mother is washing my clothes in a hurry!"

I could no longer remain seated. As I stood up and was about to leave, Yongying stopped me. "The residents' committee will meet in your house this afternoon," she said. "And you will be absent. If there's anything I can do, please tell Aunt Chen to give me a word."

I said, "My mom only told me she was occupied this afternoon; she didn't tell me the residents' committee would meet in our house. She had expected me to look after my little brother and sister for her, so please keep an eye on them for us."

"Don't you know Aunt Chen has just been elected vice-president of the residents' committee?" Yongying asked. "She's really vigorous! These days, she's been occupied with activities such as the anti-nuclear arms signature campaign and the patriotic public health campaign. My mom has told us to help her out in case she's too tired!"

I picked up my books and ran home. Mother was about to wash my uniform; I took it from her and said, "You needn't wash it; I can still wear it. There's one more thing. You have a meeting this afternoon, so I have asked Li Yongying to look after my little brother and sister for me. Please be assured of it!" Then, I ran into the inner room and hastened to make the beds and put the things on the table in order. I was about to sweep the floor of the outer room when I looked up and saw Mom looking at me by the door, her face wreathed in smiles of surprise and joy. "Xiaoqin," she asked. "How come you are so diligent today?"

Embarrassed, I blushed and lowered my head. "From now on, I'll help you out every day, my good mother!"

The Little Orange Lamp

It happened more than a decade ago.

On the afternoon before the lunar New Year's Day, I went to see a friend of mine in a suburb of Chongqing. She lived on the top floor of the village office building. A flight of dark, narrow stairs led to a room in which a table and several bamboo stools stood and a telephone hung on the wall. Beyond this room, separated by a mere cloth curtain, was my friend's room. She was not home. On the table by the window was a note she had left, saying that she was out for something urgent and that she wanted me to wait for her to come back.

I sat down at her table and picked up a newspaper. I was reading the paper when I heard the wooden door of the outer room creak open and, a moment later, someone dragging a bamboo stool. I drew back the curtain and saw a girl of eight or nine with a thin, pale face and short hair, her lips blue with cold, her clothes worn-out, and her feet sockless and in straw sandals. She was climbing onto the bamboo stool for the telephone receiver on the wall. Apparently startled by the sight of me, she withdrew her hand.

"Are you going to make a phone call?" I asked.

She nodded as she went off the bamboo stool. "I want to speak to Dr. Hu of... Hospital," she replied. "My mom spat out a lot of blood just now!"

"Do you know the phone number?" I asked.

She shook her head and said, "I wanted to ask the telephone service for it..."

I immediately searched the directory beside the telephone and found the number of the hospital. Then I asked her, "If the doctor is on the phone, where shall I tell him to go?"

"You just tell her that Wang Chunlin's wife is ill, and she will come," she replied.

After I made the phone call, she thanked me gratefully and was ready to go home. I stopped her and asked, "Is your home far from here?"

She pointed outside the window and said, "It's right under that large yellow fruit tree in the valley; it takes no time to get there." With these words, she went thumping down the stairs.

I went back to the inner room and read the newspaper from the first page to the last, and then I picked up the Three Hundred Tang Poems and went through half of it. It grew darker outside, but my friend was not back yet. Feeling bored, I stood up and looked out of the window. Through a dense fog that obscured everything in the mountain, I saw the hut under that yellow fruit tree. Suddenly, I felt like paying a visit to that little girl and her sick mother. I went downstairs and bought a few big oranges at the door. Having put them into my handbag, I went along the rough, winding stone path and arrived at the door of the hut.

I knocked softly at the wooden door, and the girl I had met opened it. She seemed a little puzzled when she raised her head and saw me, but soon she smiled and beckoned me to go in. The hut was small and dark. On the plank bed against the wall her mother was lying flat on her back, eyes closed, probably asleep. Bloodstains were visible on her quilt. Her face turned to the wall, I could only see tangled hair across her face and a large coil at the back of her head. Beside the door stood a small charcoal stove, on which lay a small earthenware pot from which a thin cloud of steam was rising. The little girl offered me the small stool in front of the stove, and she herself squatted down beside me, looking me up and down.

"Has the doctor been here?" I asked softly.

"Yes," she said. "She's given Mom a shot... She's very well now."

As if to comfort me, she added, "You can rest assured. The doctor will come again in the morning."

"Has she eaten anything? What's in the pot?" I asked.

She smiled, "Sweet potato gruel – our New Year's Eve dinner."

Remembering the oranges I had brought with me, I took them out and put them on the low table beside the bed. Without a word, the girl picked up the biggest one, pared the rind off the top with a knife, and rubbed the rest part of it gently in her hands.

"Who else is in your family?" I asked in a low voice.

"There's no one else; my dad's gone somewhere else..." She did not finish, but scooped out the

orange segments one by one and put them beside her mother's pillow.

The stove fire was dying, and it was getting dark outside. I stood up and wanted to leave. She held me back, and deftly linked the opposite corners of the bowl-shaped orange rind with a big needle and flaxen thread, thus making a small basket, which she hung on a little bamboo stick. Then, she took a candle end from the windowsill, placed it in the orange rind basket, and lit it. She passed me the lamp and said, "It's dark outside and the road is slippery. Let this little orange lamp light your way up the mountain!"

I accepted it in admiration and thanked her. She saw me to the door. I did not know what to say. Again, as if to comfort me, she said, "My dad will be back soon, and then my mom will be well." She drew a circle in the air with her little hand and then pressed her hand on mine. "And we will all be well!" she said. Obviously, her "all" included me.

Carrying this delicate little orange lamp, I walked slowing up the dark, wet mountain path. The orange-red light was too dim to provide much illumination, but I was inspired by the calmness, courage and optimism of the little girl, and I felt as if there was infinite light before my eyes! My friend had come back and, seeing me with the little orange lamp, asked where I had been. "I've been to... to Wang Chunlin's," I replied. She was surprised. "Wang Chunlin, that carpenter? How did you come to know him? Last year, some students from the medical college down the mountain were taken for communists and arrested. Shortly after, Wang Chunlin disappeared. It was said that he had been carrying messages for those students..."

I left the village that very night and, since then, I have heard nothing about the little girl and her mother.

However, I think of that little orange lamp every lunar New Year. Twelve years have passed. The girl's father must have been home long ago. And her mother must have been well, I suppose? For we are "all" "well" now!

A Performance of Dances

— Dedicated to the Indian dancers, the Kalama Sisters

How shall I describe the dances of the Kalama Sisters from India?

If I were a poet, I would write a long poem to depict their ever changing posture and movements.

If I were an artist, I would paint their fine, delicate features and gorgeous costumes.

If I were a composer, I would convey their swift steps and jingling bells in notes.

If I were a sculptor, I would reproduce their slim and flexible figure with stones.

However, I am none of these! I can only describe their spectacular art in flat, monotonous language.

I am like a baby who, seeing a dazzling red lotus in the morning sun or a peacock dancing in the forest, wants to express his happy astonishment but who can't find proper language apart from some babbling sounds.

But, friends, do you expect me to suppress my joy and excitement and refrain from "babbling" to you about my feelings?

I do not dare to pose as a scholar on Indian dance and elaborate on the history and schools of Indian dance, or prove that the Bharatanatyam they performed is a legitimate form of Indian dance. Nor do I dare to admire, like a dancer, their gesture and movements in a professional way.

I am merely a viewer, but I would love to try my best to express in words the flowing beauty I feel in my heart.

Friends, on an unforgettable evening –

As the curtains rose slowly, we saw a small table in the middle of the stage, on which stood a statue of Shiva the Cosmic Dancer. There was a lighted long-stemmed bronze lamp on both sides of the table. There was a solemn atmosphere on the stage.

Kalama Lakshman walked onto the stage. What a stunning appearance! She put her palms together before her and bowed low to the audience. As she raised her head, we saw a beautiful face and wonderfully expressive eyes and long brows.

She stood there elegantly.

There came a flute solo, then drumbeats, then

someone singing, and now Kalama began to dance.

She conveyed the joys and sorrows in the poem by means of her brows, eyes, fingers, and waist; of the flowers in her coiled hair and her pleated skirt; and of her quick short steps, jingling bells, slow movement like a floating cloud, and quick spinning like a whirlwind.

Although we didn't know the plot of the story, her gestures and movements had managed to strike a sympathetic chord in us! Now she knitted her brows as if in great sorrow; now she gave a beaming smile, expressive of infinite music; now she turned sideways and closed her eyes in seeming coyness; now she opened her eyes wide, as if in great wrath; now she simulated making up, applying a bindi to her forehead and penciling her eyebrows with gentle movements; now she stood upright, in the position of drawing a bow and ready to shoot an arrow, and we could virtually hear the twang of the bowstring! Amidst the ecstatic dances, she forgot both the audience and herself. She was completely absorbed in using her agile, skillful limbs and facial features to narrate a beautiful ancient Indian story.

When they had performed all their dances

(Lada, the younger one, sometimes did a solo and sometimes danced with her elder sister. She is definitely a talented girl! She looks very young but already displays remarkable skill. No doubt she is highly promising.), we found that apart from gods and man, they depicted nothing but plants and animals, such as a blooming lotus, a scampering fawn, and a striding peacock – all these they had imitated vividly. The most spectacular was the "Snake Dance": slight shaking of the neck, gentle vibration of the shoulders, little wriggling movement passing off and on from the fingertips of the right hand to those of the left one.

The dances performed by the Kalama Sisters give us a much deeper understanding of the beautiful and age-old Indian arts: dance, music, sculpture, painting, etc. All of which, like the branches of a huge banyan, send out roots that grow down into the soil, where all the new roots are interconnected and where they absorb nutrition provided by the Earth Mother, which refers to the people of India, a country with a long history.

Kalama and Lada are but two tender branches of this huge banyan. Although the twenty-two-

year-old Kalama has a stage career of seventeen years – and even the twelve-year-old Lada has performed on the stage for four years – we know that the great Indian Earth Mother will continue to provide nutrition for them.

It is most disheartening that, as soon as they have exhibited their dancing skills – which resemble "flying dragons" – before the Chinese audiences, they have to fly back, "quick as a flash," to their homeland in a couple of days at the request of their fellow citizens.

In the early spring in Beijing, it is difficult to find such fragrant blooms as can be found in their hometown in South India. So we have to content ourselves with imitating the poetic lines of their great poet Tagore: Let us string our admiring and grateful hearts, like little red flowers, onto chains and hang them round their necks to be brought back to the Indian people, in appreciation of their friendship and warmth and of their great kindness in sending the Lakshman Sisters here!